"By the way y'all were jumping around before, I'm guessing you made the squad?" Tommy asked us.

I nodded. "I think the herkie made the difference."

"The herkie?"

I was tongue-tied. Why on earth had I said that?

"It's a cheerleading move," Holland explained.

"Sounds dangerous," Tommy drawled.

"That depends." Remembering my new cheerleader status made me suddenly feel bold. "You've got to do it right."

Coach Prescott blew sharply on his whistle. "We've gotta get back to practice," Tommy said. "Congratulations."

"Thanks," I said lamely.

"By the way, Shauna," Tommy said as he turned to go, "what's your last name?"

I swallowed hard. "Phillips. Shauna Phillips."

"Well, hey, Shauna Phillips. Think you could give me your number? Because I just might want to learn how to do the herkie over the summer . . . and I definitely want to do it right."

If this day wasn't already the best in my life, this moment pushed it completely over the edge.

Needless to say, I gave him my number.

Don't miss any of the books in *Love Stories* —the romantic series from Bantam Books!

Love Stories

Crushing on You

Wendy Loggia

BANTAM BOOKS
NEW YORK · TORONTO · LONDON · SYDNEY · AUCKLAND

RL 6, age 12 and up

CRUSHING ON YOU
A Bantam Book / February 1998

Produced by Daniel Weiss Associates, Inc.
33 West 17th Street
New York, NY 10011.
Cover photography by Michael Segal.

ISBN: 0-553-48591-1

Published simultaneously in the United States and Canada

Bantam Books are published by Bantam Books, a division of Bantam
Doubleday Dell Publishing Group, Inc. Its trademark, consisting of the
words "Bantam Books" and the portrayal of a rooster, is Registered in
U.S. Patent and Trademark Office and in other countries. Marca
Registrada. Bantam Books, 1540 Broadway, New York, New York 10036.

PRINTED IN THE UNITED STATES OF AMERICA

OPM   0 9 8 7 6 5 4 3 2 1

To my parents, my in-laws,
and my forever crush, Chris.

Prologue

Spring, Freshman Year

Shauna

"A<small>RE YOU</small> *SURE* I look okay?" I asked my best friend and personal fashion critic, Holland Thorpe, for about the one-millionth time. I studied my reflection in the hallway mirror and gave myself my most self-assured smile. Cheerleaders are supposed to be walking bundles of confidence, but on this morning *I* was a walking bundle of nerves. This was the day I'd been preparing for all spring: tryouts for the Falconettes, Fletcher High's varsity cheer squad.

Holland ran her fingers through her short glossy black curls and gave me a critical once-over. "You look perfect, Shauna," she proclaimed, her blue eyes scanning over the pink T-shirt, gray athletic shorts, white Asics, and matching socks that had taken me about a week to decide on wearing.

"So do you, Hol. Neat and well-groomed." We both giggled. Holland's mother, an authentic southern belle, was always telling us that everyone from boys to cheerleading coaches liked girls who were "neat and well-groomed." Considering that Holland was both a cheerleader and a boy magnet, I was starting to think that Holland's mother could be right.

As usual Holland looked impeccable, dressed in navy blue bike shorts, a white knit top, and slightly scuffed white leather gym shoes. Even though it was eighty degrees out, she hadn't even broke a sweat on her bike ride to my house, and her creamy white skin showed no signs of stress-related breakouts. Holland wasn't the tiniest bit worried about tryouts . . . unlike me.

But I was attempting to psych myself up. If I was anything, I was ready for tryouts. I'd done everything all the cheerleading experts suggest: I'd had a good night's sleep (not counting the hours I *couldn't* sleep because I was worrying so much). I'd eaten a high-energy breakfast of cantaloupe, bananas, and two cereal bars. And I'd drunk about a gallon of water to make sure my vocal cords stayed nice and moist. But those were just the easy tasks.

Holland and I had been practicing together for weeks. Normally you had to be a junior to be a varsity cheerleader, but a few years ago there had been a sophomore who was so good, they'd given her a slot on Fletcher's varsity squad. And then they began letting incoming sophomores who passed an initial screening try out for varsity. To my amazement I'd passed the varsity screening, and of course so did Holland. She was a junior varsity cheerleader this year. Although being on the JV squad didn't exempt her from varsity tryouts, Holland's making the varsity squad was a sure thing. Once on the squad you could pretty much guarantee your spot there for life. Unless you did something stupid, like ram your car into the cocaptain's new BMW, which actually happened last year to some unlucky—and now ex—cheerleader.

Holland grabbed my hand. "You're going to knock 'em dead, Shauna. Think of all the time we've spent practicing. The coaches are going to love you."

I nodded, a fresh surge of determination running through me.

We stepped away from the hallway mirror and walked out my front door into the blazing South Carolina sun.

Now was the time to see if our pom-pom prep work paid off.

My heart was just about pounding out of my chest when we walked into the Fletcher High gymnasium, home of the Mighty Falcons. I couldn't believe how many girls were trying out. Sure, the tryout clinics had been crowded, but I'd had no idea the turnout would be this high. Considering our high school had over one thousand students, I guess I should have expected it.

"A lot of competition," I muttered to Holland, licking my lips.

"Yeah, too bad they're up against us," she shot back, reaching over and giving my upper arm a light punch. "We're gonna rock."

We went over to the sign-in area.

"Welcome to tryouts. If you'll just join the girls on the other half of the gym, we'll call your number when we're ready for you," said Shelley Pierce, one of the squad's cocaptains, when I finished writing my name. Shelley had run a few of the cheerleading try-out clinics I'd attended and had given me a lot of honest feedback about my abilities. Seeing her there made me slightly more comfortable. She handed me a safety pin along with a piece of paper with the number thirty-nine printed on it. "Pin this on your shirt."

I smiled. "Thanks, Shelley," I said, walking away.

"The tension is killing me," Kristen Baumgardner whispered nervously as we joined her and Liza Klevin on the other side of the gym. Kristen and Liza had been in a couple of my classes that year.

"That's part of the whole deal," Holland told us knowingly. "If you can deal with this pressure, you can definitely handle people in the stands who try to rattle you. They don't want stress cases for cheerleaders."

I looked at Holland admiringly. You had to respect the girl. She was always so poised, so together. And her confident attitude had nothing to do with her being on the JV squad already: I knew she'd be just as optimistic even if this were her first cheerleading tryout ever. In addition to being utterly cool, Holland was a very upbeat person. She had one of the most positive outlooks of anyone I knew.

After about half an hour the tryouts began. The gym was painfully quiet. Holland went before I did, and from what I could see from my uncomfortable position on the grimy gym floor, she was flawless. She'd spent a lot of time on her routine, and her execution was right on.

"You did great," I mouthed, catching her eye as she walked gracefully away from the performance section.

She grinned, her cheeks flushed from exertion. "So will you," she mouthed back.

The tryout consisted of four parts: a current group cheer with two varsity cheerleaders, a dance routine Shelley had taught us during clinics, and a thirty-second cheer we'd choreographed ourselves, after which we had to demonstrate our technical ability by doing a cartwheel and a move of the judges' request. I was sure Holland had done it all perfectly.

"Numbers thirty-nine, forty, and forty-one, please," called out Mrs. Creselli, the senior cheerleading adviser. My heart started beating faster—thirty-nine, that was me. Taking a couple of deep breaths, I walked purposefully to the judging area, trying to ignore my shaking knees. *Okay, pull yourself together, Shauna. Remember, don't look nervous. The judges hate nervous.*

Putting on my biggest smile, I performed the group cheer and the dance routine along with my fellow competitors. Then, alone, I did the cheer Holland had helped me choreograph. As I executed each move I kept my mind focused, my arms straight, and my smile bright. At one point in the group cheer I messed up, completely forgetting a line in my cheer song and missing a beat in the choreography, but I just kept on smiling, making sure to keep eye contact with each of the judges. *Maybe they didn't notice,* I thought, chewing the inside of my lip. But maybe they did. I tried not to think about it.

Then we each did a cartwheel. The other girls, sophomore Carrie Dale and junior Rayanne Nelik, seemed pretty good. A tiny trickle of jittery sweat slid down my back.

"Number thirty-nine, we'd like to see you do your cartwheel again, please." Smiling, I stepped forward and did it. Butterflies were starting to zoom around my stomach. "Number forty. Can you do a round off, please?" Carrie did it perfectly.

We stood there for several excruciating seconds that seemed like hours. Mrs. Creselli whispered something to Shelley. Shelley nodded. "Number forty-one, you can sit down," she called out. *Why did they ask Rayanne to sit?* I wondered anxiously. Was she so bad they'd eliminated her? Or had she been so good they didn't need to see her do anything else?

"Numbers thirty-nine and forty, we'd like to see you each do the herkie."

The herkie was a really hard jump. I'd hoped they wouldn't ask us to do it for tryouts. But they had, and now I just had to do my best. I took a deep breath.

Yes! I cheered silently to myself as I nailed the jump. My smile got about ten times wider as I moved back to my place in the line. Carrie wasn't so lucky. She looked sloppy and uncoordinated. I felt bad for her but hopeful for myself.

And twenty minutes later, when they called my number—along with Holland's and six other new girls'—we screamed so loud, you could have heard us in Raleigh.

I was a cheerleader!

Mrs. Creselli and the other advisers gave us all a pep talk about confidence and doing your best. She congratulated those of us who made the squad and offered condolences and tips to those who didn't. The new squad members were to meet at the gym that Friday to go over summer practice schedules and talk about the possibility of attending cheer camp.

Dismissed to go, Holland and I stumbled out of the heavy metal gym doors, jumping and crying and screaming. The warmth of the sun spilled over us, making us even giddier.

"We made it!" Holland whooped.

"We made it!" I echoed back, flinging my arms around her. We did a little dance of Falconettes' celebration.

Then, out of the corner of my eye, I saw it. The beautiful blond head of hair that could only belong to one person, one person whose every move I knew by heart. Fletcher's golden boy himself, sophomore Tommy Jansen.

"It's him," I breathed to Holland as we untangled ourselves. That was all I needed to say for Holland to know who I meant. I'd only been talking about Tommy for, oh, six months or so.

I'd had it really bad for him the last half of this, my freshman, year. I spent my days hoping to catch a glimpse of Tommy in the hallway, and I spent my nights either bemoaning the fact that I didn't see him or discussing every little detail of him if I did. I'd been watching him for so long that I felt like I knew him, even though we'd never even exchanged a mere hello.

But I knew so much about him. Like how he had a habit of giving his lock an extra spin before he did the combination. Or the way he kept a stash of junk food (usually Lay's KC Masterpiece BBQ) in his backpack's zippered pocket. The cute way his eyes crinkled in the corners when he laughed. The small brown freckle behind his right ear, perfectly situated on his slender, lightly tanned neck. I knew Tommy by heart. Although we'd never had a class together, we had shared a study hall this past spring. The high point of my day was 10:15 to 11:05, believe me.

Right now the baseball team was practicing over in Stryder Field, which lay adjacent to Fletcher. I didn't know much about baseball, but Tommy must have done something well because Coach Prescott slapped him on the back a few times and laughed. I watched spellbound as, like some scene from a TV movie, Tommy shaded his eyes with his hand and looked over at us.

Then cold fear gripped my heart. He was still shading his eyes, but he and a tall, dark-haired guy were moving. Toward us.

"He's coming over here!" I squeaked, hurriedly smoothing a few wayward tendrils away from my face. I sniffed. "I'm all sweaty!" I cried. After I had practically lain prostrate in front of him for the past six months, why did he have to pick *now* to walk in my direction?

"Relax," Holland commanded sharply. "You may not be neat and well-groomed, but . . . you *are* a cheerleader."

That got us both to giggle and jump up and down all over again. I couldn't believe I had made it! But then I noticed that Tommy and his teammate had jogged over to the nearby drinking fountain. I snapped back to reality fast.

"I'm so thirsty," Holland said mischievously, clutching her throat.

"Hol, no," I protested behind gritted teeth. But it was no use. I watched in horror as Holland strolled over to the fountain. I had zero intention of following her—until I realized she might say something to Tommy that would utterly embarrass me. Not that Holland would try to sabotage me or anything . . . but after forcing her to listen to me gush about Tommy for the last few months, I knew I had pushed her to the brink of best friendom. Holland would do anything to make my Tommy dream a reality. I hurried to join her before anything damaging was said.

"Man, it's a hot one today," the dark-haired guy with Tommy was saying to Holland.

Holland nodded. "I know. And it's supposed to get even hotter." Then she turned to me—of course she knew I'd follow her—and smiled. "Shauna, this is Cody Parker. We had sixth-period study hall together last semester. And this is his friend Tommy. He's a sophomore." She stepped back, waving her hand with a flourish as if Tommy

9

were a new sofa on *The Price Is Right.*

"Hi," I said shyly, trying to fight back the blush that was creeping into my normally pale pink cheeks. I went through a mental list of ways that I could torture Holland later.

"I've seen you before," Tommy said, looking at me. "Your locker's near mine, right?"

"Um, I'm not sure," I fibbed, trying not to look totally humiliated. Our lockers weren't anywhere near close! Mine was in a completely different section of the school. But Tommy had good reason to think my locker was near his, I realized guiltily. After all, I'd practically set up stakes outside his locker.

"So what's going on?" Tommy asked us. He gestured to the open gym doors. Girls were in huddled masses all over the place. I'd never seen so many smiles and tears in my life.

"Cheerleader tryouts," I replied, trying my best to keep my voice level at a normal octave range. If I'd thought my heart was pounding loudly before, it was practically smashing through my chest cavity now. Sure, I'd been this close to Tommy before, but never in a face-to-face conversation.

"Oh." He smiled, his white teeth nearly blinding me with their brightness. "By the way y'all were jumping around before, I'm guessing you made the squad?"

I nodded. "I think the herkie made the difference," I told him, immediately regretting my words when I saw the look of confusion on his gorgeous face.

"The herkie?"

I was tongue-tied. Why on earth had I said that?

10

"It's a cheerleading move," Holland explained, rescuing me.

"Sounds dangerous," Cody drawled.

"Yeah," Tommy added, his green eyes twinkling at—I was pretty sure—me.

"That depends." Remembering my new cheerleader status made me suddenly feel bold. "You've got to do it right," I said flirtatiously.

Just then Coach Prescott blew sharply on his whistle. "We've gotta get back to practice," Tommy told us, jerking his thumb toward the field. "Congratulations."

"Thanks," I said lamely, trying to think of something clever to say before he walked away.

Cody shot Holland an optimistic glance. "Maybe I'll see you around this summer."

She tilted her head coyly to the side. "Maybe."

"By the way, Shauna," Tommy said as he turned to go, "what's your last name?"

I swallowed hard. "Phillips. Shauna Phillips."

"Well, hey, Shauna Phillips. Think you could give me your number? Because I just might want to learn how to do the herkie over the summer . . . and I definitely want to do it right."

If this day wasn't already the best in my life, this moment pushed it completely over the edge.

Needless to say, I gave him my number.

Holland and I spent the rest of the afternoon at the beach, watching the waves lap the shore and the seagulls swoop down in attempts to secure a bite to eat.

"Sophomore year's going to be incredible," Holland declared, leaning back on her elbows onto the soft white sand.

I'd already forgiven her for bringing me to the edge of crush humiliation and back again. "Yeah. And I have a feeling this summer's going to be pretty killer too," I said happily, closing my eyes and enjoying the feel of the sun beating down on my face.

I couldn't help but smile as I thought of the days that lay ahead. Summer days that I had thought would be spent hanging out at the mall or working on my tan were now filled with a whole new world of possibilities.

Slowly the reality of the recent miraculous events was beginning to sink in.

I was a Fletcher cheerleader.

And I had finally, after all this time, caught Tommy Jansen's beautiful emerald green eye.

One

Fall, Sophomore Year

Shauna

"I'D LIKE SHAUNA Phillips and Jeff Carter to stay after class today, please," Ms. Slater announced as the bell rang, signaling the beginning of first lunch. I turned and gave Jeff, a slightly overweight boy who sat in the row next to me, an uneasy glance. He shrugged back.

Ms. Slater had passed out Monday's math tests at the beginning of class. I'd struggled through that test and had expected a grade somewhere in the seventies. Possibly even a sixty-five. But when I slowly turned up the corner of my facedown paper, a big red forty-five hit me in the face. A forty-five! I'd never done so badly in my life! To make matters worse, Ms. Slater had announced how pleased she was with the results and that only two people had scored below a sixty-five. When she asked Jeff and me to stay after, the identity of those two people wasn't too hard for the rest of sophomore math, period three, to figure out.

"Shauna, Jeff, you both failed the test." Ms. Slater opened her cowhide grade book and moved her finger down a page, stopping at two different points. "You've both done passably well on the quizzes so far this term. But this test is a major part of your grade, and failing it is definitely going to hurt your average." She turned to Jeff. "Can you tell me why, all of a sudden, your grades would drop like this?"

Jeff looked down at his feet. "My mom has been kind of sick. She was in the hospital last week getting all these tests done, and I was with her most of the time."

Ms. Slater's eyes clouded over with sympathy. "I'm sorry to hear that. Is she doing better?"

Jeff nodded. "Yeah."

"Good. I'm glad. Some things are certainly more important than math," Ms. Slater conceded. She patted her grade book. "If you can improve by the next test, we'll see about changing this grade."

"Thanks," Jeff said.

"All right." Ms. Slater smiled. "You're free to go now." Jeff nodded and headed out the door.

Then Ms. Slater switched gears to me. "So what about you, Shauna?"

I swallowed. I really didn't have much of an excuse at all. "Well, I've kind of had a lot going on since school started, and I had planned on studying more for the test, but . . ." My voice trailed off.

"Your mind seems to be elsewhere during class. Is that true?"

I paused, biting my lip. My mind was where it had been for most of last year . . . on Tommy. Except now I actually had a reason to be thinking about him. We were, gulp, going out. When a month had passed after cheerleading tryouts and he still hadn't called, I'd written him off as a number dangler. A guy who gives you false hopes. But in the last week of July, miracle of miracles, he called. I was heading off to cheerleading camp, and then he was headed off on a family vacation. But when he returned at the end of August, we got together, and we'd been hanging out ever since. Somehow school had slipped into a far recess of my mind . . . and I was in no hurry to move it to the front. Especially when it came to math.

I'd always enjoyed math, but for some reason geometry was giving me a really hard time. I tried to listen in class, and I always took lots of notes, but when I got home, the problems in my book looked a lot different from the ones we did in class. And pretty soon even opening my math book became such torture that I gave up on it completely.

"I'm trying, Ms. Slater," I told her. "It's just that I get stumped when I'm doing my homework, and I don't know how to figure something out. And I *have* been really busy lately. It's kind of like you said earlier," I confessed, "some things are more important than math."

Ms. Slater sighed, gathering the homework assignments on her desk into a neat pile. "I don't think that's what we're talking about in your case, Shauna. I will assume that your intentions are the best and that you do want to pass this class."

I nodded, hoping she was feeling generous. "Oh, I do, Ms. Slater. I really do."

"Can you stay after school on Tuesdays or Thursdays?" she asked. "We could go over your assignments, brush up on things you might be having difficulty with."

My shoulders sagged. "I wish I could," I said ruefully. "But I've got cheer practice those nights."

"Ahh. Cheer practice." Ms. Slater put the pile of assignments into her bag. "And I'm not free the other nights: My son is waiting for me in day care. But I think this will help." She handed me a stapled note that she'd obviously written before class. "I'm afraid I've got to inform your parents of your situation before it gets any worse. It's almost October. You'll have a big exam coming up at month's end. If your grades continue to fall, we'll need to schedule a parent-teacher conference."

And I'll need to schedule a road trip, fast, I thought, my stomach dropping. *Because Mom and Dad are definitely not going to be pleased to get a call from Ms. Slater.*

"I can't believe I got a forty-five," I said, furiously ripping open a bag of Doritos in the Fletcher cafeteria. *What does it matter, though? I'll be dead after I show the letter to my parents anyway,* I thought glumly.

"I can." Holland examined her slice of pizza and then put it back on her tray.

"What's that supposed to mean?" I asked, hurt.

"Well, your mind hasn't exactly been on school lately, Shauna. I mean, you're not burning the midnight oil studying, are you?"

"Not really," I admitted. "But come on," I added, making a face. "Tell me that when you're really into some guy, you don't forget about school too."

Holland pulled off a piece of pepperoni and popped it in her mouth. "There's nothing wrong with being into a guy," she agreed. "But—"

"Nothing wrong with that at all," a familiar male voice said from behind.

I turned, surprised. "Tommy!"

He leaned over and kissed me quickly on the lips. "Mr. Quinn let us out early from biology, so I thought I'd stop by to see you."

I beamed up at him, my bad mood evaporating like a puff of cheap mousse. Tommy was the hottest-looking guy in the sophomore class, maybe the whole school. Having him kiss me in private, let alone in front of the entire cafeteria, was still a little breathtaking even after being with him for almost a month. Today he looked especially cute in a short-sleeve striped velour polo and a pair of faded jeans.

"So what's this about being into a guy?" he asked, straddling the seat next to me.

I traced an imaginary line up Tommy's arm. "Holland and I were just talking about priorities."

"Yeah? I hope I'm at the top of your list," Tommy said as he waved hello to a couple of people at the next table over.

17

"That's the problem," Holland commented, taking a sip of her milk. I shot her a dirty look, and she raised her eyebrows innocently. Holland wasn't the beat-around-the-bush type.

Tommy popped one of my Doritos in his mouth. "What do you mean?" he asked between munches.

I squeezed Tommy's hand. "I, uh, I didn't do too well on my math test, and Ms. Slater gave me a note to give to my parents." I swallowed hard, feeling the weight of my math problems on my shoulders once again. "They're going to be really angry with me."

Tommy laughed. "That's what you're worried about? So throw out the note and tell Slater how it is—how busy you've been with cheerleading and after-school clubs. Teachers dig extracurricular stuff."

I sighed dramatically. "That might work for you since you're on the football team, but for us regular people life's a little tougher," I teased. And I didn't want to lie to my parents either. Of course, I didn't tell them *everything*—a person's got to have some privacy—but what I did tell them was always the truth.

Tommy stretched and stood up. "Well, if your parents freak, tell them you'll study more." He gave my hair a playful tug. "And then when they think you're studying, we'll be cruising down to the beach instead."

"Tommy," I scolded, trying to sound stern. Tommy had a habit of not treating things seriously enough unless it was something he considered crucially important—like football, baseball, or basketball.

"Don't worry too much about it. I'll call you tonight," Tommy told me, bending down and whispering in my ear.

"Okay." I reached up and touched his right dimple. "See you."

I watched Tommy as he sauntered through the cafeteria and out the wide archway into the hall. I was finally beginning to stop feeling like I was going to pass out every time he touched me. Being with Tommy was like nothing I'd ever felt before. Not only was he my first real boyfriend, but he was so popular that being with him was like being with a celebrity.

Time had moved so quickly these past few weeks that I still couldn't quite comprehend the whole thing. To be honest, my life was pretty out of control. During the day I was in school. In addition to juggling schoolwork and club obligations, I had cheer practice on Tuesdays, Thursdays, and Saturdays, and now that the official football season had started, games on Friday nights. Holland and I usually hung out after practice. And Tommy and I had been spending plenty of time together as well.

Too much time, I guessed, thinking back to my conversation with Ms. Slater. But how could I not?

"I'm only young once, right? I shouldn't have to spend every minute of my day studying!" I declared vehemently, thinking out loud.

"Not every minute," Holland agreed. "But maybe at least three or four."

I threw my empty Doritos bag at her. "Seriously, how am I going to face my parents?

They'll kill me when they read this note."

Holland shook her head. "No, they won't. Think positive."

I rolled my eyes. She would say that, wouldn't she?

I waited until dinnertime to spring the news. Luckily my parents seemed to be in pretty good moods that night.

"Can you believe it? We're booked solid for the next six weeks. The autumn tourist season is really becoming a phenomenon," my father said, helping himself to more tossed salad. He managed the SeaSpray, a huge hotel right on the ocean in Myrtle Beach. His job was pretty demanding, and he didn't always get the chance to eat dinner with us. I was glad he was here this night. When it came to arguments, I could usually count on him to be on my side.

"Wow, Dad, that's fantastic," I said, smiling sweetly. Then I wiped my mouth daintily with my napkin and stood up. "By the way, Ms. Slater wanted me to give you this." I gave my father the note.

"What is it?" asked Lindsey, my seven-year-old sister. "An invitation?"

"No, not exactly," my father said, reading the note carefully. Too carefully, I noted.

"Frank, let me see that," my mom said, putting on her bifocals.

My dad handed it over to her. "Ms. Slater says that your grades are falling, Shauna. Why didn't you tell us you were having trouble with math?"

I looked down at the tile floor. "I don't know. I didn't think it was that bad."

"You're spending too much time with Tommy, Shauna," my mom chided, looking up from the note. "And now it's catching up with you."

"I am not!" I protested hotly.

"Your mom's right. You've always been a good student, Shauna." My dad nodded disappointedly. "Too much socializing," he said firmly. "Cheerleading and schoolwork and Tommy—you need to get your priorities straight. You're going to have to cut something out. And—"

Not wanting to hear what I knew was bound to be bad news, I spun on my heel, ran down to my room, and slammed the door so hard, the walls vibrated and my dried rose bouquet fell onto my floor. In my heart of hearts, I knew my parents were right. I did have a problem. A big one. But just like the ones I faced in math class, I didn't know how to solve it.

Thirty minutes later there was a knock on my door.

"Come in," I mumbled, flopping over on my bed.

My mom peeked her head in. "Honey, I think we've come up with a solution to your problem." She came inside my room. "We're getting you a tutor."

I looked at her blankly. "A what?"

"A tutor," she repeated. "A math tutor."

Was she joking? I shook my head. "No way. No way am I getting a tutor."

My mom pulled a piece of lint off her blouse and tossed it into the garbage can next to my desk.

"It's already taken care of. Dad left a message on the answering machine of the student center that Ms. Slater recommended. He said you'd be in to start tomorrow afternoon."

"Mom!" I shrieked, slamming my fists down on my bed. "How can you guys do this to me?" I wasn't stupid. I'd just been spending so much time with everything else, I'd kind of let school take a backseat for a while.

"We're not doing anything to you." My mom gave me one of her looks: eyes like steel through her glasses, hands planted firmly on her hips. "You're the one who got yourself in trouble, Shauna. Not us."

A tutor? Visions of sitting in a cramped-up study carrel with my math book and some geek wearing flood pants while Tommy strolled home with a girl on each arm filled my mind. *I would have waited for you, Shauna, but you were in the middle of an equation with Alfred. Sorry. . . .*

Desperately I tried to come up with a reason, an excuse, to get out of this nightmare. "None of my friends have tutors! That stupid tutor center is for nerds."

I knew that was pretty lame. But the thought of actually going into Brain Drain (the name alone was enough to kill you)—no, of actually being seen walking in there—was more than I could bear. I crossed my arms. "I will *not* go there!"

"Fine," my mom said, her voice crisp. She turned to go. "I'd better call Mrs. Creselli."

I scrambled up off the bed. "Why?"

"Because you'll have to quit the cheering squad if

your grades don't stay up. It's early enough in the season, though. I'm sure they'll be able to find someone to take your place," she called over her shoulder.

I sat back down, defeated. My mom was right. That was one of the bylaws of the cheerleading squad. All FHS cheerleaders had to maintain an overall average of at least B–. I was doing pretty well in social studies, science, and English. But I wasn't doing so hot in French (thank goodness Mrs. Glassman didn't send home warning letters). A C in both math and French could definitely put my cheerleading days in jeopardy.

I was between a rock and a hard place. Hanging out in Brain Drain would be a major negative on my social life. And I was already having a hard time juggling Tommy and school and friends and cheerleading. How was I going to squeeze in sessions with a math tutor as well?

But failing math was not an option either. Dispirited, I turned on my TV and flipped through the channels, barely registering the images that flashed before my eyes. I fingered through the stack of *Teen*s that were piled next to my nightstand. Then I walked over to my bedroom window and peered out into the dusky twilight.

There was just no getting around it.

Sighing, I padded down the hall in my matted old Tweety Bird slippers. My mom was wiping a smudge of tomato sauce off the kitchen stove, and my dad was scrubbing plates with a vengeance few plates had seen before. Lindsey was playing Barbie dolls in our family room.

"I was beginning to think you'd forgotten your

nightly duty," my mom said as I walked in the kitchen. When Lindsey had started kindergarten, my mom had gone back to work part-time at a jewelry store in the mall, and I had to help out more at home.

"Sorry." I grabbed a linen dish towel and began drying. "So," I said casually, "did you call Mrs. Creselli yet?"

"No. Why? Do you want to call her yourself?"

"C'mon, Mom. Stop torturing me. I'll go to Brain Drain, all right?" Like she didn't know I'd succumb eventually.

My mom reached out for my hand as I put a freshly dried plate down on the counter. "Honey, we're not torturing you."

My dad flicked a cluster of soapsuds at me. "Shauna, this isn't just about cheering. You might not think so now, but math is important. And if you let yourself fall behind this early in your sophomore year, you'll be headed for real trouble down the road."

I nodded mutely and picked up a dripping glass. "I know. But—but . . ." I faltered. "I just don't want people thinking I'm stupid!" I blurted, a tear falling down my cheek. I put down the glass. "And that's what everyone's going to think when they see me walk in there!" Not to mention I wouldn't be able to be with Tommy as much. I hoped my friends would remember me . . . because I didn't think I'd be hanging out with them for a long, long time either.

My mom came over and put her hands on my shoulders. "Oh, Shauna. Is that what you think about the kids you've seen going into Brain Drain?"

I shrugged, shaking a tear off my face. "I don't know. I guess I've never actually paid attention to them."

"There you have it," my dad replied confidently. "No one is going to care at all that you're going in there. And if they do, who needs them? You're the smart one. People who need help and don't ask for it are the real losers."

My dad looked so serious standing there, wearing my mom's frilly yellow apron to protect his dress pants, up to his elbows in soapy water, that I couldn't help but smile. "I guess," I managed weakly.

"No more tears, honey. This isn't something to get so worked up about," my mom soothed, planting a kiss on my forehead.

I took a deep breath. "Well, I don't really have a choice about this," I mumbled. "But it doesn't mean that I have to like it."

"Fair enough," my dad acknowledged.

"How long do I have to go there?" I asked worriedly.

"Well, until you and your tutor are in agreement that you understand the material, I guess," my mom mused out loud. "In her note Ms. Slater said she thought it might take a month or two."

A month or *two?* A wave of depression washing over me, I watched my dad as he pulled the plug on the sinkful of soapy water.

That wasn't the only plug that was being pulled. So was the one on my social life. And just like the water that now whooshed down the sink, my plans for after-school romance with Tommy would soon be swirling down the drain as well.

Two

Chad

"OKAY," I MUTTERED to myself. "All this stuff fit in here an hour ago. It's got to fit in here now."

I shoved the wooden bats in the corner of the closet and put the bases on the top shelf. I'd been trying to wedge the equipment from my phys ed class into the locker-room supply closet for the past ten minutes, and my patience was running thin. Just as I was finally about to shut the door, a volleyball rolled off the shelf and unceremoniously plunked me on the head.

"Come on!" I yelled in frustration, picking up the ball and whipping it back in. This was one of my more idiotic moves—two more balls now spurted out, along with an old tennis net and a field hockey stick.

I sighed heavily, checking my watch. Three-thirty. Fifteen minutes late for my tutoring job. Why

26

did Coach Prescott have to ask me to put all the phys ed equipment away today? I shook my head—I knew why. There was a big football game that night, and Coach didn't want to risk any of his precious players—several of whom were in my gym class—getting hurt. Not that a couple of old volleyballs and some dusty bases should be considered dangerous or anything, but I guess Coach had his reasons.

Finally I managed to round up every stray ball and get the supply closet safely shut, pitying the next poor lug who opened it. At least no one besides Coach Prescott could finger me as the culprit. I'd claim innocence to the bitter end. I grabbed my backpack and jogged down the hall toward Brain Drain.

I hated to be late. Not only was it rude, but it also threw off the order of things. I'm probably one of the most orderly guys on the planet. I hang up my clothes at night, I throw out old pizza crusts (unlike some guys I know), and my most prized possession, a black '95 Eclipse, has a regular date with the local car wash on Saturday mornings. I know girls think that most guys are total slobs, and I can't say that I don't have my slob moments. But for the most part I'm a pretty methodical guy. And punctuality was at the top of my list.

I slowed down when I got to Brain Drain. The center was on our library's second level, and when you entered, you were supposed to be quiet. Our school wasn't that old compared to some—built sometime in the early eighties, it had a lot of glass

27

and weird multicolored tubes sticking out all over the place. It was actually kind of cool compared to others I've seen.

I jogged up the stairs and stopped quickly by the front desk to scrawl my name on the tutor on-call list. I was scheduled to work Mondays, Wednesdays, and Fridays after school. Being a tutor at Brain Drain was kind of a combination of volunteerism and actually working. I received a small check every week; not as much as I could have made working somewhere else, but enough to help me pay for gas and have some extra spending money. And being a tutor definitely would look good on my college applications. Besides, not to brag or anything, but I was pretty great at math, and after hearing my math teachers ask, "Have you ever thought about tutoring, Chad?" for years, I decided to take the plunge.

And I guess it was a good thing because I was always booked. In fact, I was probably the most popular math tutor in Brain Drain. There were all kinds of tutors here: English, science, language arts. But when it came to math, I was the tutor everyone wanted. I'd won a couple of math awards, and somehow the word had spread that if square roots and radicals were your problem, I was your man.

There was a note from Mr. Hill, the guidance counselor who monitored Brain Drain, wedged in my private mailbox. *New student. Needs to see you MWF for the next month or two. Sophomore math. Her name is Shauna Phillips.*

I crumpled up the note and air-balled it into the

garbage can. "Score!" I whispered loudly. Lizbeth Fisk, one of the other math tutors, gave me a high five. Then she looked up at the clock.

"You're late."

I raised my eyebrows. "Can't you cut a guy some slack?"

Lizbeth tilted her head toward the study carrels. "Sure, *I* would. But that cheerleader is starting to get really mad."

"Huh?" I asked, furrowing my brow. "What cheerleader?"

"Your new client. Shauna something. She's been waiting for you ever since classes let out."

I grimaced. "Oops." I grabbed a couple of pencils, a blank pad of paper, a folder of loose-leaf geometry work sheets, and an eraser. "Time to get crackin'."

"Yeah, and by the way," Lizbeth stage-whispered, smiling, "I like your outfit. Very trendsetting. Don't see many like it roaming the halls."

I looked down at my clothes as I walked away. Great. In my haste to get the baseball stuff put away, I'd forgotten to change. Now here I was in my droopy blue-and-white Fletcher High Falcons shorts and an old white tank top with a Falcon iron-on crumbling off the back. Oh, well. I might be a sweaty, smelly mess, but I still knew my stuff.

All the tutors had their own unofficial study carrels. Mine was on the far right of the room, adjacent to the glass wall that looked out over the football field. It was pretty peaceful, really. But that day as I approached, I heard this weird tapping sound. Like a little woodpecker was pecking away at the glass or something.

A pretty girl with long wavy brown hair wearing a short flowered skirt and a fuzzy purple sweater was sitting at one of the two chairs at my carrel. There was a pile of books in front of her and a co-ordinating backpack next to her feet. She was tapping her pencil tip against the white tabletop in sharp, quick motions.

"Hi. You must be Shauna. I'm Chad Givens. I'm really sorry to keep you waiting."

"I was beginning to wonder if you were going to show," she said, looking up at me, a slight tinge of annoyance in her voice.

I put the pencils, eraser, folder, and pad down on the tabletop, which was covered with about a thousand pencil dots. "I realize I'm a couple of minutes late," I said apologetically. I could feel my already flushed cheeks turn even redder.

"Seventeen minutes, to be exact," Shauna informed me. "For someone who's supposed to be good with numbers, stuff like that matters, right?" Her brown eyes, sparkling with mischief, lingered on me. "Did you stop to take a quick workout or something?"

I sighed. "Look, this really isn't my day."

"Mine either." She wrinkled up her nose. "I think I've got some Shower to Shower in my locker. I can go get it if you want."

"I think we'd better just get started, if you don't mind. We don't have much time as it is."

"All right." She moved her chair over slightly to make room for me.

"So, Mr. Hill tells me that you need help in math. Is that right?" I clicked on the overhead study carrel light.

She sighed. "Yep."

"What book are you using?"

"Uh, here." She pulled out a heavy book from the stack in front of her. It was wrapped in a brown paper bag book cover and covered with stickers and ink drawings of peace signs and hearts. *Connected Mathematics: Course I.*

I nodded as she held it up. I knew it like the back of my hand. "Well, what exactly is the problem?"

"My grades are going down, and fast. I just failed my math exam, and Ms. Slater sent a warning letter home to my parents." She moaned. "I have *got* to bring this grade up and pass my next exam." Now void of mischief, her eyes bored into me like a dart gun.

I tried to smile. I hated when people expected a miracle cure after only one session. "Well, according to Mr. Hill, you're set to meet with me on Mondays, Wednesdays, and Fridays from three-fifteen to four-fifteen. If those times ever pose a problem, we can try to set something up where we meet at night."

She shook her head emphatically. "That won't be necessary. A short session after school is fine. The shorter the better, really. I'm superbusy these days," she confided.

I could see this wasn't going to be easy. "Okay,"

I said slowly, "but we will have to meet for at least an hour. We don't tutor anyone for less than that amount of time."

Shauna sighed again, a long, painful sigh. "Fine."

"Well anyway, usually what I do is help students with their daily homework and then give out some additional work sheets to work on at home and turn in to me at our next session."

Her jaw dropped. "You're giving me *homework?*"

"That's how it works," I replied, trying to sound completely impartial. "After a few weeks you'll get used to it."

"I don't know about that. I'm having trouble just finishing the homework from class." She hesitated, then snapped her fingers. "You don't have a quicker method? You know, like speed-reading but for math? I mean, you are a smart person, after all. You probably have something like that here, right?"

Now there was a new one. I gave a snorting laugh. "No, not really. You're going to have to put in some time if you want to do well, Shauna. You can't cut corners when it comes to math."

Foiled, she drummed her fingers on the tabletop impatiently. Then she leaned forward, her elbows on her bare legs and her long hair spilling over her shoulders. "Look, I'm sure you're a very nice person and everything, but I've got to level with you here, Brad. Math is not my top priority."

"Really," I said, feigning surprise.

"No. Well, yes and no. I mean, it is for now, but it won't be for long." She twisted a strand of hair around her finger. "See, I just made cheerleader, and if I don't keep up my grades, Ms. Slater will notify the selection committee and I could be forced to quit the squad." A dreamy expression appeared on her face. "And I just started going out with someone this summer, and he takes up a lot of my time. You know how it is."

"Yeah, right," I agreed with her, as if my romantic involvement was seriously infringing on my spare time. "Relationships'll do that to you."

She nodded emphatically. "I'm glad to see that we're on the same wavelength, Brad."

"Chad."

"His name? Tommy. Tommy Jansen."

I frowned. "No. *My* name. It's Chad. Not Brad."

Shauna laughed. "Sorry."

I quickly read through her assignment for the weekend and asked if she had any questions about it. "I know we're running out of time, but I'd be glad to stay a little while longer if you'd like," I said. "To make up for being late," I added generously.

She ran her fingers through her long hair and peered out the glass window. All of a sudden her face lit up. "That's nice of you, but I really can't. I've got to go home and grab some dinner before the game tonight."

"Oh, right. Well."

"So," she said, quickly gathering up her things. "I'm to read over my assignment and we'll go over it on Monday?"

"Mm-hmm. I also thought you could use this."

I handed her a sheet of paper. "We've got a Web site for Brain Drain students. You can visit the site and drop us a line to say hello or to let us know that you're having a problem. And you can communicate with other Drainers—you know, ask them questions or help them with theirs."

"Drainers. Uh, thanks," she said, taking the paper from me as if it were the plague. She shoved it in her backpack, barely giving it a glance. "Okay. See you on Monday, then. Bye!"

"Bye."

I sat there for a moment, thinking. Shauna was certainly one of the more bubbly students I had worked with in recent months. It was hard to say if she was going to study hard. But it was no sweat off my back, really. I got paid whether or not she learned the material. Of course, I always hoped that my students would finally get the concepts their parents were paying for them to learn.

A minute later I realized I'd forgotten to give her a work sheet. She'd probably blow it off anyway, though. Grabbing an apple out of my bag (we weren't supposed to eat in Brain Drain but no one ever said anything to us), I leaned back to stretch my legs. My eye caught a glimpse of something purple outside the window. It was Shauna, walking over toward the bleachers. I watched as one of the football players came over to her and gave her a kiss. He said something to her then and she laughed, her head tilted back and her wavy hair blowing slightly in the breeze.

Feeling a bit like a Peeping Tom, I averted my

gaze. I took out my copy of *Of Mice and Men*, the novel we were reading for English, and opened it up to where I'd left off last night. Shauna was probably right. I guessed it would be hard to concentrate on something like schoolwork when you were in love with someone.

Luckily for me I didn't have that problem.

Three

Shauna

"**H**AVE YOU HEARD? We'll spread the word. The Falcons are here. *F–A–L–C–O–N–S.* Go, Falcons!" I yelled, lifting with my shoulders and pushing through my toes as I jumped. Then, along with my squad mates, I dropped to my knees and extended my left arm above my head, keeping it close to my ear, and placed my other hand sharply on my hip. The punch motion always fired up the crowd, which, as expected, roared its approval.

A rush of pride ran through me as I looked up into the stands, spotting some of my friends laughing and joking. It was a perfect autumn night for a football game: The temperature was in the low sixties, and it was early enough in the fall to be light out still.

From the other side of the line Holland winked at me, her hair pinned back with tiny blue-and-white barrettes. I looked down at my navy-and-white sweater and matching skirt with the metallic gold

36

accents, *Falcons* emblazoned across the front, and grinned. This was what cheerleading was all about.

I focused on Erica Terry, the team's cocaptain along with Shelley. When she gave the signal, we lined up in our dance formation position. I always liked the dance numbers. Not only was I a pretty good dancer, but I felt more comfortable with the cheers that focused on dancing rather than tumbling. And we always danced to good music to pump up the crowd even more.

Tonight as I went through the motions of the dance, my mind turned to Chad Givens and the tutoring session of that afternoon. If you could even call it a session. I mean, not only did I have to wait around for someone who supposedly got paid by the hour, but then he showed up all sticky and sweaty. He seemed nice enough, I guessed, but I'd bet he'd be a big drag. We weren't together for more than forty-five minutes and the guy was already giving me homework!

I was sure we had nothing in common. Chad wasn't in any of my classes, and I didn't recall ever seeing him at football games or at any of the school clubs I belonged to: the Magnolia Blossoms dance squad, the international cultures club, and Teen to Teen, the teen crisis hot line.

And I'd never seen a guy so shy before. His face had turned about a hundred shades of red during our session. If he was that way with all the girls he tutored, his face must be in a perpetual state of sunburn! Not that his face was unattractive. His eyes were nice and his smile sincere. He was actually kind of cute in a tutorial way, but I—

"Shauna!" Rayanne Nelik hissed.

"Wha—" I'd been so caught up in my little tutor session rehash that I'd kept doing the dance routine while everyone else had grabbed their pom-poms and headed for the bench. I conked myself on the head. "Duh! Thanks, Rayanne!" I said gratefully. To my relief no one seemed to have noticed.

"Who do you think you are out there, Miss Thang?" Holland teased as I hurried over to the bench. She scooted over. "You have got to stop thinking about Tommy so much. It's written all over your face!"

"It is?" I poked her in the ribs. "Well, then your mind-reading abilities are failing, because he was not what I was thinking about." Holland's always saying that she can read people's minds. And actually she's guessed a few things about me that have made me wonder if she really can. But when you think about it, we've been best friends for the past four years or so—if she doesn't know what's on my mind by now, who does?

Holland carefully tucked her pom-poms under her legs. "So who were you dreaming about, then?"

"I wasn't dreaming about anyone. I was just thinking about the tutoring session today. About my annoying new tutor."

"Anyone I know?"

"Doubt it. His name's Chad. He's a junior."

"Chad Givens?" Holland perked up.

I nodded, surprised. "Yeah. You know him?"

Holland nodded back. "We were on student council together. He was the treasurer."

I rolled my eyes. "Naturally. He's a dweeb. And I'm going to be stuck meeting with him for three days a week."

"A dweeb?" Holland shrugged. "That's not the person I'm thinking of. About my height, long light brown hair, brown eyes, wire-rimmed glasses. Cute in a bookish way."

"He wasn't wearing glasses," I told her primly, briefly thinking back to his eyes. "And his hair is not long."

"Well, anyway, he seemed pretty nice from what I remember."

"Then maybe you should go out with him," I said playfully. "I might be able to find some time between triangles and line segments to ask him if he's available."

Holland shook her head. "Like Mark would be cool with that." For the past two weeks Holland had been sort of seeing this senior, Mark Muffitt. Tonight he was home, sick with the flu. "Hey," Holland said, nudging me. "Looks like you're up."

I glanced at Erica and Shelley on the sidelines, did a few quick stretches, grabbed my megaphone, and ran out to join them. One of my favorite things was when we did the special players' cheers. The key varsity football players all had a special cheer just for them, and anytime they did something spectacular, we usually performed one. It was understood that if any of the cheerleaders was dating any of the key players, that cheerleader got the chance to cheer for her guy.

I held up the meg. "Tommy, forty-three, Tommy, forty-three! Yell it! Yell it!" The crowd complied, and I repeated my chant a few times. Then I leaped into the air, bringing my right leg straight up and extending it out to the side, my right arm bent and my fisted hand on my hip. At the same time I bent my left leg, bringing my foot back toward my rear hip, making sure to keep my knee down. It was the herkie, my trademark jump for Tommy.

My voice really carried when I used the megaphone, and Tommy turned at the sound, his shoulders looking impossibly huge in his football jersey and his legs looking taut and lean through his pants. He held up the V for victory sign and gave me a wave. I waved back.

If things stayed as they were, it looked like I'd be doing the herkie for a long, long time.

"Did you see Jansen run?"

"The Falcons *creamed* them!"

"State championships, here we come!"

The home crowd was abuzz with excitement. Everyone had expected the Falcons-Tigers game to be close, but Fletcher had hammered them 35–10. It was an incredible win—a win made possible by Tommy's stellar performance on the field. Not only had he run for two touchdowns, he'd also caught the pass for the last touchdown in the fourth quarter. He'd been named the game's MVP.

Holland, the rest of my squad mates, and I gathered outside the Falcons' locker room. It was FHS tradition to wait for the players to come out, especially after a victory.

"Tommy was totally awesome out there," Rayanne told me admiringly.

"Yeah. You are *so* lucky," chimed in Natalie Smith, a curvaceous junior with straight blond hair. "I mean, the guy's pure eye candy."

"Thanks," I said, my cheeks glowing with happiness. I rubbed my hands together in an attempt to get them warm. It had grown quite chilly in the past hour.

"How long have you guys been going out?" asked Claire Ulrich. She was one of the quietest cheerleaders on the squad.

"Almost a month," I replied.

"So are you, like, really serious?" Natalie prodded. I smiled and shrugged. We hadn't discussed what exactly we were, but neither of us was seeing anyone else.

"Of course she is," Rayanne told her, as if it were obvious. "Who wouldn't be serious about Tommy?"

"I'd keep my eye on Nat the Cat," Holland whispered in my ear as Natalie walked away. "She's after Tommy."

"And the *rest* of the football team as well," I whispered back.

All of a sudden the people around us started going crazy: jumping up and down, yelling, throwing blue-and-white confetti in the air. The Falcons had begun to stream out of the locker room.

"Tommy!" I called, spotting him.

He made his way through the throng of well-wishers, his duffel bag slung over his shoulder, his hair damp from the shower. With him were his two best friends and teammates, Lance Roval and John Grisaldi, and John's girlfriend, Chrissy.

"Hi, Shauna, Holland," Lance and John said in unison. Chrissy gave us a small, strained smile. She was convinced that all the cheerleaders were after John, and her paranoia made her stick to him like glue.

"Hi," I said, then turned my full attention to Tommy. "Congratulations!" I gave him a huge hug. "You were incredible."

"Nice work out there," Holland added.

Tommy bent down and gave me a kiss on the lips. My mouth tingled slightly at his touch. . . . His kisses still felt new. "I heard your voice from all the way out in the field," he kidded.

I grinned. "That's because I was yelling at the top of my lungs."

Mr. and Mrs. Jansen materialized and immediately began showering Tommy with well-deserved praise. "We're really proud of you, son," Mr. Jansen said, slapping Tommy on the back.

Mrs. Jansen beamed. "My Tommy, MVP!" She gave him a hug and lovingly rumpled his hair. "Don't celebrate too hard tonight," she cautioned, pinching his cheek. "You keep your eye on him, Shauna."

"I will," I said, smiling. Unlike my parents,

who demanded to know my every move and whereabouts, the Jansens belonged to the school of "we trust you, don't tell us—just stay out of trouble." Tommy was pretty much free to come and go as he pleased, a freedom that seemed incredibly grown-up to me.

We waved good-bye as the Jansens stopped to brag with some other parents who were congregating outside the locker room.

Blissfully I linked my arm into Tommy's strong one, and together we followed Holland out of the school doors. In the parking lot we were thrust into a huge, noisy crowd of football players, girlfriends, cheerleaders, and various parents and adults. Everyone stopped to congratulate Tommy. It took us a full ten minutes to get to the car.

"Yo, MVP!" yelled a group of guys. "See you at Carlo's."

Tommy grinned, his eyes twinkling. "You got it," he called back.

"Forty-three, you *rule!*" another overzealous student cried before hopping into a souped-up Camaro and peeling out of the parking lot.

When we got to Tommy's Blazer, he popped open the back and he, Lance, and John threw in their dirty uniforms and duffel bags.

"You're going to Carlo's?" I asked, surprised. Tommy hadn't mentioned anything about that to me. Carlo's was a great pizzeria—one of my favorites, in fact. They had the best brick oven pies I'd ever had. I didn't get to go there very much, though, since it was in Conway, about fourteen miles from the section of Myrtle Beach where I lived. I didn't have my license yet; I wouldn't be sixteen until January.

Tommy clucked me under the chin. "*We're* going to Carlo's, Shauna. Man, I'm starving."

Lance, John, and Chrissy piled into the back of the Blazer, and Tommy stood waiting for me by the unopened passenger door. I held up my wrist, straining to make out the numbers on my watch in the murky black Carolinian night. It was nine-thirty. "How long do you think we'll be at Carlo's?" I asked, wondering if I would be able to make it home before my 11 P.M. curfew.

Tommy shrugged. "Why?" he asked. "You gonna melt or something?" Lance and John laughed. "What's the problem?"

I hesitated. "Well, I was kind of planning on studying tonight after the game." That was the truth too. I had that big math test coming up, and if I didn't do well, my whole life would probably fall apart at the seams. "And you know about my curfew . . . ," I reminded him.

"You can't be serious," Lance said, sticking his head out the window. "We just *annihilated* the Huston Tigers and you're going to let a *curfew* stop you?"

Tommy nodded. "Yeah. I mean, you've gotta come to Carlo's, Shaw," he implored, using the nickname he'd given me at the beginning of September. "Everyone's going to be there." He reached out and took my hand. "You don't want me

44

to be lonely, do you?" His emerald green eyes were all big and puppylike, and he wore such a sorrowful expression that he made me giggle in spite of myself.

"What about you, Holland?" Lance asked.

"'Fraid not," Holland told him. She jingled her car keys. Holland had turned sixteen on September 19, and her driver's license was burning a hole in her pocket. "I'm heading over to Mark's house with some homemade chicken soup. And I've got to get the car back to my house before ten or my parents'll freak." She turned to me. "Why don't you ride home with me if you don't want to stay?"

From the corner of my eye I saw Chrissy giving John a nudge. Nervously I chewed my lip. For months I'd wanted nothing more than to be part of Tommy's life, and now here I was turning down the chance to be with him after the most important football game of his career . . . and for what? Math class? I'd already fallen so far behind that missing one night wouldn't kill me. *You can always squeeze in an hour or two of homework after the pizza,* my devilish side whispered in my head.

"I guess I could study sometime tomorrow or Sunday," I said slowly, trying to convince myself that what I was saying was actually in the realm of possibility. I had cheerleading practice the next day from eleven to two, a date with Tommy that night, and I was supposed to baby-sit Lindsey on Sunday while my parents went to a hoteliers' gathering at the convention center.

"Sure, you can," Tommy urged. "Is one night of

45

fun going to ruin you? There's plenty of time to hit the books this weekend." Tommy pulled me close, close enough to feel his heartbeat through the thin cotton material of his V-neck shirt. "And I promise to try and get you back home before your curfew, Cinderella."

"So . . . ?" Holland prompted. I turned to her—she was looking from Tommy to me.

"Um, well, I guess I'll stay," I decided.

Tommy wrapped his strong arms around me—the arms that had just scored the final touchdown—peppering my neck with kisses. "That's my girl," he whispered. I shivered, both from the cold and from the touch of his lips on my chilled skin.

"Thanks anyway, Hol. I'll call you tomorrow." I broke free from Tommy and gave Holland a quick hug. "Say hi to Mark."

"I will," she said, heading off to her car. "Have a good time."

Without another word Tommy unlocked the passenger door and held it open for me. "We don't have to spend the whole night at Carlo's," he said softly into my ear. "Maybe we can do a little postgame celebrating on our own."

The warmth of his breath was enough to make any lingering resolve melt, and without another moment wasted I got in the car. Lance was right. There was plenty of time to buckle down and get serious. It wasn't every night that my school, with Tommy leading the way, had a killer victory over a rival like the Tigers.

And it wasn't every night that I had the cutest guy at Fletcher begging me to stay by his side.

Four

Chad

I STOOD AT attention, waiting for Master Chung's orders. It was 10 A.M. on Saturday, and I was at my biweekly tae kwon do class at Chung's School of Martial Arts. I'd joined the black–belt program there several months ago. That meant that I paid up front for almost three years' worth of classes. But I could come as often as I wanted to, which with my schedule usually amounted to twice a week. The idea was to work my way up to a black belt—it would take a lot of perseverance, but the payoff would be a tremendous feeling of accomplishment. I glanced down at the orange belt wrapped around my crisp white *dobok*. It was like I told my tutoring students: Nothing good comes without hard work. And if I wanted to be a black belt, I was definitely going to need to work hard.

"Hi, Chad," a low voice greeted me to my left.

I turned and smiled. "Hi, Ralph." Ralph was an

older guy, somewhere in his thirties, I guessed. We tried to pair up together in our Saturday morning class since we were the only two guys there over the age of fourteen. The early hour scared a lot of people off. That day, besides Ralph, there were a couple of yellow-belt boys who looked around ten years old, an orange-belt woman in her early thirties, and a blond girl who was probably about eight. She was a green belt—one belt higher than I was. That was the thing about martial arts. Your age really didn't matter. It was your level of skill and proficiency that counted.

We did about twenty minutes of warm-up stretches and then Master Chung signaled that it was time to move on to the next segment of class.

"Okay," he said, clapping. "Time to jog. *Joonbi.*" Taking a deep breath, I fell into place in front of what probably was a third-grader and began to jog the perimeter of the room. I wanted to be a black belt badly, but sometimes I wondered if I was a glutton for punishment.

After we jogged around the dojo for about fifteen runs, we spent the rest of the class doing forms and a bunch of regular drills. Master Chung varied the class from session to session. You never knew what he was going to do next.

Next we practiced our forms for our next belt level. The green-belt form was a little tricky, and I ended up having to ask Marie, the little blonde, for help. Then Master Chung had us do ten minutes of a kicking drill—running up and kicking pads that

48

he held in front of him. By the time we finished with some light contact sparring, *kyorugi,* I was ready to collapse. Only the thought of meeting my best friend, Jamie, after class and the burger I would soon be devouring kept me going.

The last few minutes were spent in meditation. Master Chung played soft, relaxing music, and we sat cross-legged on the floor, letting our bodies hang limp and our minds go free.

I closed my eyes, relishing the feel of the good workout I'd just put my body through. It was worth every moment of sweat and fatigue. My body had improved over the past few months: My legs felt stronger, more flexible. My lung capacity had increased too; now I could run three miles without becoming winded. I was definitely getting in shape—I'd even had a couple of whistles from a passing car of college-age girls as I was jogging the other day.

Girls. I sighed inwardly. For some reason I hadn't had much success in that department. Then again, I'd never really tried. I'd always been so into my schoolwork that girls had kind of taken a backseat. But lately I'd been rethinking my situation, and I was wondering if maybe I couldn't find a little time to spend with the opposite sex.

I'd just have to find the right girl to spend it with.

The Riverboat Café was home to the best burgers in Myrtle Beach. Maybe in all of South Carolina. The place wasn't much to look at, but that was part of its charm. There were license plates tacked up all over the walls, and big dishes of peanuts graced every table—tables that were peppered with good-natured graffiti, like Sally Loves Mike or Spring Break '98: TKE Rules! Jamie and I had made an agreement that we had to eat here at least once a week. And since Jamie's family's condo was only a couple of blocks away, he was able to keep up his end of the bargain and more so.

Jamie Manning and I had been friends since junior high. He was a bit of a cutup. And he liked to think of himself as God's gift to women. With his buzzed black hair, quasimuscular body, and outgoing personality, his thinking probably wasn't too far off.

Emmy, our usual waitress, came over to our table and plopped down a basket full of steaming hot hush puppies and a crock of butter. She gave Jamie a weary look. "The regular?"

Jamie's eyes twinkled. "You know I've got to say it."

Emmy groaned. "Spare me. Just once, spare me."

I rolled my eyes. Jamie thought he was Mr. Hilarity or something. Every time we came here, he ordered the same thing, in the exact same way. He denied it, but I was certain he had a thing for our tall, red-haired, thirty-something waitress.

"I'll have the crab cake, cupcake."

Emmy nodded. "Somehow I could have guessed. And for your less annoying partner in crime?"

I hesitated. "The smothered cheeseburger. With onions."

"Onions?" Jamie wrinkled his nose as Emmy walked away. "You better not be breathing on me later."

"Darn." I sighed. "There goes this afternoon's plans."

Jamie popped a hush puppy in his mouth. "So, you testing for your green belt yet?"

"Nah. Master Chung pretests us when he thinks we're ready for the next level. He hasn't pretested me yet." I took off the piece of paper that kept the silverware and the napkin intact. "Besides. I've got a lot of work to do before I'm ready for a green belt. I mean, I still have to learn a new form, and make sure I've got the kicking motions down right from my last form, and—"

"Hmmm," Jamie mumbled, barely listening to a word I'd said. A tall leggy blonde wearing a jean miniskirt and halter top had just walked by our table, and Jamie's head was swiveling out of control. "Did you see that?" he said, choking on his Coke. "She was incredible!" Then he looked at me and shook his head. "Oh, I forgot. Looks aren't enough for you."

I took my wadded-up straw wrapper and shot it directly at Jamie's face. He was always giving me a hard time about girls. Just because the one girl I'd really liked a few years ago, Marcy Miller, had won our middle-school spelling bee three years running and took a prize in the eighth-grade science fair, Jamie thought that brains were all that counted for me. He had it all wrong. Sure, I wanted to meet a smart, terrific girl. But I also hoped she'd be attractive. Was that too much to ask for?

Jamie had gone out with this one girl, Sara, for two years. Jamie had been crazy about her. But then

51

they grew apart and Jamie wanted to start seeing other people, so they agreed to break up. The truly tragic thing about this was that Jamie now considered himself an expert on love and doled out advice whether I wanted it or not.

"So how was the game last night?" I asked, changing the subject. Jamie and our friend Phil went to almost every Falcons game. For me, rooting for the Carolina Panthers was enough. I didn't get into high-school football in quite the same way.

Jamie rubbed his hands together excitedly. "Awesome! We won thirty-five to ten. Our team's really got a lot of power this year." He leaned back as Emmy deposited our food in front of us. "And man, the cheerleaders looked awesome. That Shelley Pierce, she could join my team anytime."

I took a big bite of my burger. It was just how I liked it: well-done to the point of being almost burned, cheddar cheese oozing down the sides, and crunchy onion slices rounding off the top. "Speaking of cheerleaders, I'm tutoring one," I said between bites. "Shauna Phillips."

Jamie clutched his crab cake sandwich. "Wait a minute, Givens. You've got your mouth full, but I could swear you just said you're tutoring Shauna Phillips."

"That's what I said."

"She's gorgeous!" Jamie exclaimed. "Man," he muttered, shaking his head. "Why do you get all the luck?"

I laughed. "You always say that tutoring's got

to be the world's most boring job. Now all of a sudden I'm lucky?"

"If you get to be alone with Shauna Phillips, then I'd say you're pretty darn lucky."

I took a sip of my Coke. "Jamie, it's not like that. We're there to study, not to hook up or anything." For some reason Shauna's softly lashed brown eyes and flower-shaped mouth suddenly flashed into my mind. "Anyway, she's got a boyfriend."

Jamie sat up straighter. "You asked her if she had a boyfriend?"

I reddened. "No. *She* mentioned him to me. In between running her fingers through her long brown hair," I added jokingly.

"You guys were talking about dating!" Jamie slapped the table. "See, I knew it wasn't all about schoolwork." Then he gave me a funny look. "What's the matter?" he asked, staring at me.

"Nothing," I said, feeling self-conscious.

"No, no. Something's the matter." His eyes grew wide. "You like this girl, don't you?"

"Of course I do," I hedged. "She seems very nice."

Jamie gave me a fixed look. "No. I mean, you *like* her."

I rolled my eyes. "What makes you say that?"

"Oh, I don't know. Maybe because in the six years I've known you, you've never once mentioned a girl, let alone her *long brown hair!*" he howled. Several diners turned to look at him. "That's great, man, that's great. Too bad she's got a boyfriend. But who knows? Maybe they're not that serious."

53

I cleared my throat. "Well, I think they are serious, Jamie, but that doesn't matter because I'm really not interested." I stared at him. "Believe me."

Jamie shrugged and tossed an empty peanut shell onto the floor. "Whatever you say, bud." Then he winked at me. "But the truth is out there. And I know it."

On Monday afternoon I made sure to be in my study carrel at three-ten. *That'll show her,* I thought self-righteously. *Chad Givens is never late . . . unless he has a good reason.* I laid out two precisely sharpened number-two pencils, a thick pile of scrap paper, a calculator, a ruler, and my Chewbacca eraser. Shauna couldn't accuse me of being ill prepared today, that was for sure.

Grabbing a piece of scrap paper, I began doodling a trapezoid. I was just getting ready to shade it in and add a smiley face when a large thud jolted me.

"Hi," Shauna said breathlessly, dropping her books on the study carrel.

"Hi," I said crisply. "Have a seat."

She looked thoughtfully at the carrel. "If you wouldn't mind, I think I'd feel more comfortable sitting on the floor."

"Well, okay," I said, trying to be adaptable.

"My back's been bothering me today, and stretching out always helps. We do a lot of stretching in cheer practice," she explained.

I shuffled through some papers, barely glancing at her. It had been my experience that new students often tried to trail off on other topics just to avoid the inevitable dreaded problem they were there to address. "Let's get down to business. Your homework for today?"

She brushed away some imaginary dirt and sat down on the floor, handing her notebook to me. "Here are the problems from pages sixty-eight through seventy."

I quickly skimmed them over. "Not bad," I said approvingly. She had done several problems perfectly. A self-satisfied smile appeared on her face. "But it would have been nice if you'd finished *all* of them." I stared down at her. "You can't really just pick and choose here, Shauna."

"I did the first ten!" she protested, her smile vanishing.

I tapped my pencil impatiently on the carrel. "Yes, but the first ten are also the easiest. That's how they structured this section. To warm you up with the easy questions. Then when you feel confident, they hit you with the harder ones. Harder problems call for different strategies than easy ones."

"Oh. Well, you should have mentioned that," she objected darkly.

"Here, why don't you open your book to page sixty-eight and we'll go over the ones you didn't understand together."

Shauna opened her book and propped it on her stomach. Then, to my dismay, she began doing leg lifts.

"Shauna, if you want to learn, you're going to have

to concentrate. And you can't concentrate if you're lying there doing exercises." I paused. "Can you?"

"I like to study this way," she countered, lifting her right leg into the air and holding it there for a moment. "I do my best work like this."

I'd seen my share of rotten study habits, but this took the cake. *Fine. If it'll make her learn easier, whatever.* Going along with her, I went over her assignment. I was surprised to see how much Shauna really knew. It was apparent that if she'd just put a little more effort into it, she would have finished her entire assignment correctly.

"Wow," she said as we finished up her homework about fifty sets of leg lifts and thirty minutes later. "Ms. Slater just went over this whole thing, but I didn't understand a word she was talking about. You made it so much clearer!"

I smiled modestly. "Well, I try."

She sat up. "Am I free to go now?"

"Just a minute." I walked over to one of the Brain Drain bookshelves and returned with a cluster of work sheets.

"Practice makes perfect," I said, my eyes twinkling at the look of horror on her face as I gave them to her. "They're not as bad as they look," I added. "Have them done for Wednesday."

"*What* a day," Shauna proclaimed, falling into the study carrel seat beside me two days later. "I'm wearing new shoes, and my feet are killing me." She held up her feet, which were wedged into a pair of blue sandals.

Relieved to see that she had decided to use a chair today, I scanned through my notes from Monday's session. "Okay. You were going to do the work sheets, and then we were going to go over your homework assignment."

Shauna frowned. "Work sheets? I don't remember anything about work sheets."

I frowned back at her. "I gave them to you at the end of our last meeting, remember? I asked you to try them, and you shoved them in your backpack," I continued, trying to jog her memory. How could she have forgotten?

Shauna chewed her lip. "Oh. Let me see." She fished around in her backpack, pulling out a tube of lipstick, a water bottle, a pair of tennis shoes, and a pack of gum. Then she pulled out several crumpled sheets of paper. "Oops." She attempted to smooth them out on the table in front of us. "They got a little wrinkled."

"Looks like it," I said in my most neutral voice. Brain Drain tutors were supposed to encourage their pupils, not put them down in any way or be negative. "I guess you're going to have to save them for next time." I gave her a hopeful smile. "You do have your homework done, right? I mean, of course you do. You just came from math class."

She fished through her bag once again. "Here it is," she said proudly, waving a notebook in front of my eyes. Before I could blink, she'd shoved it back in her bag.

"Uh, Shauna, it would help if I could actually

see your work. It's easier to go over it that way."

"Oh." Reluctantly she took out the notebook and handed it over. "These are the problems from pages seventy-three through seventy-five."

"Okay. Let's see what you've got." I flipped to the corresponding page in the text. Unlike on Monday, today she had a big nothing—not one answer was right. Not only that, none of the answers made the remotest sense at all.

Problem 1:
Given the premises: $a \rightarrow c$
$\sim a \rightarrow b$
$\sim c$
Prove the conclusion: b

Shauna had scrawled: $x = y$.

Problem 2:
Apply the chain rule to the given set of
premises to write a valid conclusion:
If I live in Sacramento, then I live in California.
If I live in California,
then I live near the Pacific Ocean.

For this one Shauna had come up with, "If I visit California, I will not go to Sacramento."

I took off the wire-rimmed glasses I sometimes wore for reading and rubbed my eyes. Then I looked at her. "Is this some kind of joke?"

"What are you talking about?" She bristled.

"I'm talking about the fact that all your answers are wrong."

She folded her arms. "That's why I'm here. I need help."

"But the other day you really seemed to have caught on. I don't understand."

She didn't respond, her mouth drawn in a sullen pout.

Frustrated, I leaned back in my chair, tilting it to that precarious position between balance and embarrassment. "Shauna, I'm here to help you—not do your work for you. I can't help you if you won't cooperate. You didn't even bother with the work sheets. And from the looks of it, you didn't read your math homework."

Shauna fidgeted uncomfortably with her pencil. "It's not that I don't want to cooperate," she mumbled. Then she flung the pencil against the carrel wall, breaking its pointy tip. "Some of us aren't brainiacs, Chad. I have a life, you know. I can't just spend all my time reading about theorems and logic and stuff."

"Then why are you here?" I pressed.

"For someone so smart, you're pretty dumb. I need *help!*" she burst out. "And you're doing a lousy job of helping me."

I knew I was kind of a bookworm. A brainiac, to use Shauna's lingo. But that was a label I put on myself. To hear someone else call me that was frankly a little annoying. And then she had the gall to insult my tutoring skills? *Who does she think she is?* I thought angrily. Here I was, getting paid to help her, and she was putting me down?

From across the room I saw Lizbeth watching us. I scowled back. Then, without a word, I began putting my pencils and scrap paper into my bag. "You don't need my help," I said coolly. "What you need is to actually open up your book and look at the problems on the page."

"But—"

"There's no way you read your assignment," I continued. "The homework you were supposed to do was basic, the fundamentals of logic." I scratched my head, trying to come up with a way to make her understand how important this was. "The chain rule is vital to every single branch of mathematics: algebra, geometry, statistics. Your answers made no sense."

"You don't—"

"I have a life too," I told her thinly, standing up. "And if you applied the chain rule to what just happened today, you would conclude that my life probably shouldn't include tutoring you." I turned around and stalked out of the tutoring center. "You can get a refund at the desk," I barked over my shoulder, bearing down the aisle to the door. My blood was racing. I'd never walked out on a student before, not even a difficult one. And I'd had my share, believe me. There was just something about Shauna that set me off. For some reason I felt personally wounded by her comments.

A few seconds later I heard the thud of shoes behind me.

"Wait up, Chad."

I pretended not to hear her.

"Wait, Chad. Please?" Shauna came up puffing alongside me. "I'm sorry. I wasn't trying to be insulting or anything." She held up her hands apologetically. "You caught me, okay? I didn't have time to do my homework. There was the football game, and—"

I cut her off. "Save your excuses, Shauna. I really don't care." When it came to tutoring, I was pretty much a hardnose.

She stopped. "I didn't do my homework, and during homeroom I filled in the blanks with . . . with . . . any old thing." Shauna hung her head. "Give me another chance?"

As I looked at her as she pleaded with me, my heart did an unexpected flip-flop. Shauna looked so pretty standing there, her eyes big and soulful, her lips slightly parted. And she was wearing these slightly flared, formfitting jeans. . . .

I jumped, startled, as she reached out and touched my sleeve. "I promise I'll work hard, Chad," she said earnestly. "I won't blow it off. I really need your help."

I shot her a quizzical look and tried to snap back to reality. "Really?"

She nodded emphatically. "Really."

I stood there, trying to ignore her delicate hand on my arm. It was against my better judgment to continue. I seriously doubted Shauna's change of heart. She'd probably goof off every time we met, and I'd be getting paid to do basically nothing, to tutor someone who wasn't even remotely interested in improving her math skills. But as I looked at her, I just couldn't say no.

"All right," I told her grudgingly. "But there are a few ground rules that you've got to follow." I paused, trying to come up with some off the top of my head. "It's my way or the highway," I said gruffly. I'd heard that line in a movie once, and I'd been dying for a chance to use it.

Her contrite expression turned to one of amusement. "I told you, Chad. My feet are killing me. The highway just isn't an option."

Five

Shauna

FOR THE NEXT twenty-four hours I lived and breathed mathematics. I hadn't intended to put so much time in, but I had made Chad Givens a promise that afternoon, and I was sticking by it. Not to mention that I had to prepare for the upcoming math test, which loomed over me like a never ending equation. And when Chad had gotten angry at Brain Drain, part of me had felt guilty for slacking off. It all began with my traipsing off to Carlo's last Friday night after the game. I'd enjoyed the pizza, but with every bite I thought of what I should be doing . . . and how I wasn't doing it.

On Saturday, I'd had cheer practice until two o'clock. I'd only had time for a quick shower at home before Holland picked me up and we went to see a sculpture exhibit at Brookgreen Gardens that she was going to write about for her art class paper. Then Tommy and I double-dated with John and

Chrissy, getting heros and sodas and sitting on the beach, walking up to my dad's hotel when we were through to go midnight bowling. I'd reread my notes on Sunday, but Lindsey kept me running ragged until my parents came home.

And then after my Monday session with Chad, I'd spent some time with Tommy. Tuesday was cheer practice, and I also had a five-page English paper I was working on. I'd had all good intentions to put in the time for math, but it was like that quote my English teacher had put on the board last week, "The best-laid plans of mice and men go awry"—or something like that.

So that night after dinner, I brewed myself a big mug of coffee and made a beeline for my room, keeping the door shut and my Bush CD on low. At first I sang along with Gavin, picturing Tommy and me in various romantic scenes set to the music— but soon I had completely blocked out the music and the rest of the world, including Tommy.

I recognized some of the things that Chad had outlined that day after our rocky start. Excited, I scanned through my homework problems. They didn't look easy, but then again, they didn't fill me with that humongous feeling of dread that I'd been experiencing lately.

I frowned when Lindsey barged unexpectedly into my room. "I need the hair dryer," she informed me, waltzing over to my vanity. "Amber and I are playing hairdresser."

"Well, hurry up and get out," I ordered, staring

64

down at my paper. I'd been working on this page for the past half hour, and it was starting to get to me.

Lindsey put her hands on her hips. "What's your problem?"

"My problem?" I huffed. "My problem is, 'Find the truth values for a and b that would make $a > b$ false.'"

"Huh?"

"Exactly," I said. I shoved her out of my room and shut the door firmly in her face. By the time I turned off my desk lamp three hours later, my eyes were weary and angles, sides, and vertices were engraved on my brain cells.

On Thursday I found out that practice *does* make perfect. In math class Ms. Slater sprang one of her infamous pop quizzes on us *and* collected our assignments. But I didn't sweat a drop. I'd worked hard on my assignment, and while I might not have gotten every problem right, it would at least be evident that I'd tried. And when Ms. Slater called on me to go to the board, I walked up there with confidence.

"Very good, Shauna," Ms. Slater said after I sat down.

Matt Reynolds raised his hand. "I don't understand how she came up with that answer," he argued.

Ms. Slater looked at me. "Shauna?" Here was the true test of comprehension. Did I really know my stuff—or was I just copying it from someone else?

"Well," I said, taking a deep breath. "It's all

because of the law of simplification. See, if you extract the single statement *r* from the conjunction . . ."

I walked down the hall after class, humming the *General Hospital* theme song. For the first time in a long time, I hadn't exited Ms. Slater's class with a twisted knot of pain in my stomach. It felt so good to be called on in class and know the answer. All that time I'd spent poring over letters and numbers the night before had been worth the effort. It was like the prep work I did for cheer practice. How could I expect to do well in class if I didn't put in the necessary work outside of class?

I reached my chipped orange locker and began spinning the dial with a renewed sense of focus. Just as I opened the door Tommy appeared and leaned against the locker next to mine.

"Hi," he drawled, giving me that slow, easy grin that made my heart skip a beat. He was wearing a white T-shirt we'd picked out together at the mall. The shirt really set off his tan.

"Hi, yourself," I said, depositing an armload of books onto the locker floor. "What's up?"

Tommy reached out and put his hand on my hip, a shock of blond hair spilling across his forehead. "I can't wait to ride the bus with you tomorrow."

I looked at him, unsure. "Is something wrong with the Blazer?"

"No, dopey." Tommy squeezed my hip. "The *team* bus. It's an away game, remember?"

"Of course I do," I answered, blushing. "I just

didn't know you meant *that* bus." The cheerleaders usually relied on Mrs. Creselli and a rotating squad mother for transportation to the games. Riding on the football players' bus was by invitation only. This would be my first time on it. Except . . .

The team bus left much earlier than the cheerleaders did—so early, in fact, that I'd have to miss my session with Chad.

I hesitated. Here I was, feeling all determined and focused and proud—actually beginning to catch on. Could I really afford to skip a tutoring session? "That sounds great. But—"

Tommy nuzzled my cheek. "But what?"

The nuzzle clinched it—I'd blow off Brain Drain. The team bus was legend. No way could I pass up a ride on it . . . or a chance to be with Tommy.

"But I, um, I'll need to tell Mrs. Creselli," I finished.

"Okay. And get this." Tommy leaned in even closer in an attempt to create some intimacy in the noisy corridor. "After the game a bunch of people are coming over to my house." Tommy winked. "My parents are out of town."

Nervously I twisted a tendril of hair around my finger. "Y'all won't do anything crazy, will you?" I asked. I'd heard some wild Falcons party stories.

Tommy's left dimple twitched, captivating me. "You'll just have to wait until tomorrow night to find out, Shauna girl." He checked his watch. "I've gotta go. I won't be able to call you tonight. Me and the guys are going over some last minute plays at Rice's house. But I'll see you on the bus tomorrow at three." He leaned over and grazed my lips with his. "Later."

"Later," I whispered, kissing him back.

I nibbled on my lip as I watched Tommy walk away. Should I tell Chad the truth? He was liable to get annoyed, especially after the little lecture he'd given me yesterday about the importance of math. And what good would that do? I knew there was no way I would renege on my arrangement with Tommy. The football players' bus! I was really psyched. After all the time I had put in the day before, I'd earned a little R and R with my boyfriend. Chad would just have to deal.

I headed down the hall to Brain Drain. I'd do the right thing and leave Chad a message—I'd think of an excuse to get out of our session. It was the smart thing to do. What if Chad called my house tomorrow to see why I wasn't there? My parents would bug out.

To my surprise Chad was standing at the library's entrance. He was in the middle of a conversation with a dark-haired girl dressed in a striped tank top and faded overalls.

"Hi, Shauna. Stopping by for an extra session?" Chad joked.

I wrinkled my nose. "Negative."

He grinned. "See?" he said to the girl. "She's always thinking in positive and negative terms. I love that!"

"Ha, ha." I sniffed.

Chad motioned to the girl. "Deb, this is Shauna. She's one of my pupils at Brain Drain. Deb's a senior—she's in my Latin class."

"Nice to meet you," Deb said.

I nodded, trying not to stare at the small diamond stud that glittered in her nose. I was surprised that Chad had a friend who looked so alternative. He, well, he seemed so straitlaced. By the book. "You too," I said politely.

Chad shifted his weight from one leg to the other. "Seriously, is there, uh, something you need help with?"

"No. I, um, actually just wanted to leave you a message," I stammered. Why was I so nervous? Before I could talk myself out of it, I blurted, "I, uh, can't make our session tomorrow. I'm . . . I'm getting a cavity filled."

Chad grimaced. "Ouch."

I nodded, trying to look worried. "Yeah. See?" I opened my mouth and pointed to some vague area. "I've been putting it off for a while—I can't stand the dentist—but my mom says I've got to get it over with." That wasn't actually a lie. My dentist had been on my case; I'd just never scheduled the appointment.

"Gosh. Well, don't even worry about the tutoring session." He smiled reassuringly. "You've got a lot of potential, Shauna. We'll get there."

"You don't know the half of it," I related, filling him in on what had happened in class today. "Thanks to you there's the slim chance I'm actually going to pass sophomore math with a decent grade."

"I have no doubt that you will." Chad raked his fingers through his light brown hair. "Well, if I'm going to pass my next class, I'd better get going. Catch you later, Deb." He turned to me, a look of concern on his face. "Good luck with that tooth, Shauna. And really, don't worry about the session." He shifted his books from one arm to the other. "If you don't watch out, you'll be the best student I have. And then I'd have to get rid of you." With a nod good-bye he joined the horde of students streaming down the corridor.

"That is one terrific guy," Deb mused, her voice full of admiration. "He's so busy with tutoring and track and stuff, but he takes the time to help other people out when they're in trouble. You know, really listen to them. Now that's cool." She laughed. "Not to mention that he's got a great butt."

The older girl's first comment made me pause. I hadn't really looked at Chad as anything but a math tutor, but Deb had a point. Obviously he had a lot more interests than I knew about. He seemed like a pretty interesting person, if you got the chance to know him.

Then I reflected on her second comment. She had a point there too.

Six

Chad

"WHAT ARE YOU watching?" I asked.

My dad hit the pause button on the remote. "A tape we ordered on smart investment strategies. Mom thought it would be good to brush up on them." My parents were both accountants. They met at the University of South Carolina at Columbia, where they were both business majors. After they graduated, they were married right on campus. My parents worked together in the same accounting firm for a few years, and after I was born, they built an addition onto our house and started their own company. You'd think they'd get sick of each other, seeing as how they're together practically twenty-four hours a day, but they never seem to.

"Mmm." I sprawled out on the couch and tried to get into the tape. But it wasn't happening.

"Is everything okay, honey?" my mom asked, looking up from her blue-lined notepad. My mom's always taking notes. She says that's the mark of an organized person. Never mind that she's always writing things down and then wondering what her notes meant in the first place.

I sighed. "Yeah. I'm just kind of bored is all." Since Shauna had canceled our session for that day, I'd been able to finish my biology homework before dinner. I still had to read some short stories by Nathaniel Hawthorne and write an essay for English, but I didn't feel like doing school stuff now. I'd had enough thinking for one day. I wanted something fun. Something outdoors. Something mindless. Something to start the weekend off right.

Something like . . . like football. Jamie and Phil were always bugging me to go to the school games, and I usually turned them down. Tonight was an away game. Jamie didn't have his own car yet and Phil did, but he'd failed his driver's test twice already. So I was pretty sure they'd be home.

I went out to the kitchen and punched in Jamie's number on the cordless.

"Hello?" Jamie answered.

"You up for a night of Falcons football?"

Silence. "Chad? Is that you?"

"Yeah. I was feeling kind of restless, and I wondered if you wanted to check out the game over at Jefferson." I rummaged through the fridge as I spoke, pulling out some grapes.

A yell pierced my eardrum. "Give me ten minutes. I'll call Phil. You're a lifesaver, man!"

I didn't know if I'd go that far, but I was happy

to have a plan. After a week of school I really needed to wind down on Friday night. Lots of Fridays Jamie, Phil, and I ended up shooting hoops in Phil's driveway or watching TV at Jamie's. Jamie worked part-time at a local public golf course, and sometimes Phil and I would spend practically the whole night in the clubhouse, talking shop with Jamie and discussing the pros and cons of woods and irons. Then again, lots of Fridays we didn't do anything. I hated those nights, and they happened more often than not.

I polished off the grapes and went back into our living room to tell my parents where I was going. Then I dashed down the hall to the bathroom and brushed my teeth. I glanced at my reflection in the medicine cabinet mirror. My hair was starting to look a little ratty around the ends. I'd let it grow long last year, almost to my shoulders. But then my mom got on my back about it, and I had to agree that I did look a little derelictlike. So I'd gotten my hair cut really short. It looked great at first, but now, growing out, it had gotten a little crazy. I squeezed out a large blob of gel and rubbed my palms over my head.

I was in the sweats and mangy old T-shirt I'd put on when I'd come home from school. Now I debated whether or not I should change, finally deciding to put on a pair of old jeans, a sweatshirt, and a jacket in case it got chilly.

I hurried out the front door, not knowing why I was spending so much time getting ready. After all, it wasn't like there would be anyone to impress at a Fletcher High football game.

"I told you this was a bad idea," I muttered.

"Chill out, man. What's the problem?" Jamie said from behind me. He'd insisted we stop at the pep squad's concession stand, and as a result we were carrying three large sodas, two bags of popcorn, three hot dogs, and an order of nachos with cheese up the rickety old bleachers of Jefferson High.

"If you spill it, only the entire crowd will notice," Phil added.

"Yeah, all twenty of them," I said. I would have gestured to the stands except my hands were full. Jefferson, our host for tonight's game, was about a fifteen-minute drive from my house. There was a huge contingent of Jaguars fans, but the Falcons crowd was pretty meager.

"We'll just have to yell a little louder," Jamie said, sliding down an empty row. It was the middle of the first quarter. No one had scored yet, and the Falcons crowd was on the verge of comatose. I guess that's why the cheerleaders decided to come over and try to fire us up. We watched as they assembled down in front. Pom-poms waving, they began to cheer. "*S-P-I-R-I-T!* Spirit leads to victory. So get on up and give a scream! Shout it out for the number-one team. That's it! Go, Falcons!"

To my horror Jamie leaped to his feet. "Give it up for the cheerleaders!" Jamie cried, waving a little blue-and-white flag he'd brought with him from

74

home. "Especially Natalie!" A few people laughed. Natalie rolled her eyes, but I could tell she was secretly pleased at the attention. The other cheerleaders ignored him and took position facing the field. I shrank down in my bleacher seat.

"Whoever came up with the idea of cheerleader uniforms knew where it's at," Phil said, crunching into a cheese-soaked nacho.

I had to agree. My eyes had been drawn to Shauna and her short white pleated skirt the moment we'd sat down. She was the only cheerleader I actually knew personally besides Holland Thorpe, whom I remembered from student council. But that wasn't the only reason I'd noticed Shauna Phillips. There was something else about her too. Something special.

"So why'd you decide you wanted to come out tonight?" Phil asked me.

"To see that incredible display of spirit from Jamie, of course," I replied. I took a big handful of popcorn.

Jamie propped his legs up on the row of seats in front of us. "See all the fun you've missed in the past, Givens?"

The next few minutes were spent in silence as we watched the Jaguars defense push the Falcons back. And then, to Jamie and Phil's collective horror, the Jaguars scored a touchdown.

Jamie buried his head in his hands. "Are they sleeping out there or what? *Wake up!*" he barked. The cheerleaders hightailed it out to the field and did a quick, inspirational cheer.

I watched as Shauna and the other girls went through what looked like a pretty complicated routine. Shauna's long hair was pulled up in a high ponytail, and little blue-and-white star stickers were plastered to her left cheek. She was really yelling her heart out. I was quite impressed with the moves she was doing—they were like something you'd see on TV. I realized there was more to Shauna Phillips than met the eye as I watched her perform. She wasn't as delicate as I'd thought. . . . She was a real athlete.

I guess I must have stared at Shauna a little too long because when I looked away, I noticed Jamie and Phil whispering to each other and shooting me covert glances.

"What's so interesting down there, Chad?" Jamie asked, his eyes twinkling.

"Could it be . . . Shauna Phillips?" Phil cracked.

I felt my face redden. "I have no idea what you guys are talking about," I replied crossly.

Jamie and Phil high-fived each other. "Chad, your cheeks couldn't keep a secret if your life depended on it!" Jamie responded. He grinned. "Excellent choice, I might add. The girl's gorgeous."

At that very moment Shauna tilted her chin, her eyes grazing the very section we were sitting in. Jamie winked at me and waved.

I yanked his arm down. "Quit it!" I hissed. "Are you trying to totally humiliate me?"

Jamie shook me off. "You're just her tutor saying hello."

I growled.

"Look, man, take it from me. If you want a chance with a girl like that, you've got to make a move. I know."

Phil nodded sagely. "Our love god, Jamie Manning."

Jamie sighed and brushed his fingers against his chest, then blew them off. He'd just met this girl at the mall, and they'd exchanged numbers. She called him the following day, making his head swell even bigger than it already was. "When you're hot, you're hot."

I was just about to tell Jamie that I absolutely did *not* want a chance with Shauna nor did I need his assistance in making a move when one of the Falcons broke away from the crowd and began running toward the end zone.

"Touchdown!" Jamie stomped the bleachers as the Falcons crowd—which had grown a little bigger—erupted into a cheer. "Now we're talking! Now we're talking!"

Shauna and the other cheerleaders jumped around and hugged each other. If I'd doubted her ability to be enthusiastic about something, I was put in my place now. *I wish I could get her that psyched for math,* I thought.

For some unaccountable reason Shauna looked once more in our direction. I didn't think there was any way she could detect me in the crowd. The wind was whipping her hair around, practically covering her face, and it had started to grow dark—

I had to be invisible to her in my jeans and navy jacket.

But all the same I smiled down at her.

There wasn't any harm in being friendly.

"Man, I can't believe we lost tonight," Jamie grumbled as we headed down the steps, the rotting old wood threatening to splinter at any moment.

"It was this close!" Phil muttered, holding up two of his fingers a fraction apart.

It was unseasonably cool for an October Myrtle Beach night, and I was wishing I'd worn my leather jacket instead of my thin nylon windbreaker. As we walked out through the chain-link fence that surrounded the bleachers I heard a girl call my name.

"Chad!" she called again.

I halted and turned. There was Shauna, surrounded by a pack of laughing, chattering cheerleaders, waving at me.

"Hi," I said. As I walked over to her my lip twitched. That happened sometimes when I felt nervous. Shauna had put on a white satin jacket, but I noticed that her legs were covered with goose bumps. "You must be freezing," I told her.

She shivered. "That's the price we pay for wearing these short skirts."

"We're glad you're willing to make the sacrifice," a voice piped up from behind me.

I turned around and glared at Jamie and Phil. As usual they were bopping and clowning around. *If you even attempt something embarrassing, I will leave you stranded at Jefferson,* I told them tele-pathically with my eyes. They seemed to get the message because they straightened up and looked fairly normal, which for them wasn't easy. I turned back to Shauna.

"These are my friends, Jamie and Phil."

Shauna nodded hello.

"So, uh, not a great game, huh? Not that you weren't great," I added hastily. "You guys were the best part."

"By far," Jamie added under his breath.

Shauna kicked at the pebbly gravel that lined the walkway. "No, it wasn't one of our better games." She looked up at me, her brown eyes questioning. "I'm surprised to see you here, Chad."

"Why?" I asked. "I don't live in Brain Drain, you know," I kidded.

She shrugged. "No, that's not it. We just don't get a lot of fans at the away games."

"You should," I said. "You were really good out there. It made the game a lot more fun watching you."

Shauna smiled, and for the first time I noticed what beautiful cheekbones she had. "Thanks! It's a lot of hard work and practice, though. You have to be pretty dedicated."

"I can imagine." I stood there, trying desper-ately to think of something engaging to say be-fore Jamie butted in with some cheesy comment. "How was the dentist?" was what I came up with.

Shauna gave me a blank stare. "Oh, right," she

said suddenly, slapping herself lightly on the cheek. "I ended up not getting in. The dentist was, uh, overbooked. I had to reschedule."

"Oh." I noticed a bunch of Falcons cheerleaders piling into a minivan twenty yards from us. "Hey, I don't want you to miss your ride," I told her, toying with the zipper on my jacket. "If you need a lift home or anything, I've got my car here. Jamie and Phil are kind of obnoxious, but they're harmless creatures, I promise."

Shauna smiled at me. "That's nice of you, Chad, but I've already got a ride. I'm riding on the—"

"Hey, Shauna! What are you doing over there?" A muscular blond guy stood waiting impatiently on the football players' bus, a letterman's jacket slung carelessly across his shoulder. I recognized him as the same guy Shauna had met outside the school the other day. It was her boyfriend, Tommy Jansen.

Shauna blushed. "—bus," she finished with a laugh. "I'm sorry. I've got to go." She began to walk backward. "Thanks a lot for your offer anyway."

I shrugged. "Sure," I said, acting as if offering the prettiest cheerleader a ride home and being turned down was an everyday occurrence. "See you Monday, then."

"Right. See you Monday."

I turned around, not really wanting to look at her any longer. "Let's get out of here," I muttered to Jamie and Phil. I shoved my hands in my pockets and stared down at the gravel beneath my feet as we shuffled off to the car.

I'd realized something just then, something that was making me feel quite depressed.

It wasn't that I didn't want a chance with Shauna Phillips.

It was that I didn't have one.

Seven

Shauna

"THIS IS WHERE we lost it, right here!" Randy Choi, FHS quarterback, said definitively, flinging a pillow at the Jansens' wide-screen TV set. "I can't *believe* we did that."

"Believe it," Tommy said ruefully from his place in front of me on the floor. I rubbed his shoulders sympathetically. Wedged like I was in between Chrissy Talbot and Joy Lanphere, Randy's girl-friend, on the couch, there weren't many other options for contact.

"Where'd they get the tape from?" I whispered to Chrissy.

Chrissy pointed to Joy.

"You videotaped the whole thing?" I said, my eyes widening.

"Right down to the wire. Randy always likes to watch it after the game, see how he looked out there and stuff," Joy confided.

"That's some dedication."

"Football is everything to these guys," Chrissy said dolefully. "Believe me. After going out with John for the past year, I realize where I fall on the totem pole."

I was beginning to see what she meant. We'd been at Tommy's house for the past hour and a half, and for the past hour and twenty minutes we'd been watching Joy's video. Except we weren't just watching it straight through, which would have been palatable. Every few seconds one of the guys hit the pause button on the remote. Sometimes they varied it by hitting the slow-motion button. We were only up to the second quarter.

Yawning, I leaned my head back. My thoughts drifted, for some weird reason, to Chad Givens. It was funny seeing him at the game, out of the confines of Brain Drain. And I sensed he felt the same way—he'd acted kind of nervous. Maybe he didn't feel comfortable around all the football jocks or something. A ripple of guilt had washed over me—when he'd asked about my tooth, I'd felt like a real heel. He'd looked genuinely concerned.

All of a sudden John fell into Chrissy's lap, sending her into a fit of uncontrollable giggles. I tried to move over to avoid being squashed by John's thrashing thighs. Tommy came to my rescue, standing up and pulling me to my feet. I snuggled into him, breathing in the sexy scent of his cologne.

A heated discussion had started while my mind had been roaming off.

"Listen, you guys. The Marketplace doesn't

check ID. That'll be the best place," Tommy said decisively, running his hands through my hair.

Randy shook his head. "I don't know. I've heard they're cracking down lately. Maybe we should just forget about it."

"What's wrong with you guys?" Lance scoffed. "I'm not afraid to go."

"I'll go with you," Tommy offered. As an afterthought he turned to me. "We'll be back soon," he said, touching my cheek. "You don't mind, do you?"

"No, of course not," I said, even though I wanted nothing more than for him to stay glued to me like John did with Chrissy. As usual the two of them were locked together in deep conversation on the couch. Joy had disappeared outside. Although I knew Tommy was glad I was there, we hadn't talked a whole lot. He was so wrapped up in football that I was kind of left on my own. Not that he wasn't being nice to me or anything. But I couldn't help but feel that something was lacking. We'd made fun of John and Chrissy's tight twosome in the past, but now I saw that their closeness was something I wanted too.

After Tommy left, I wandered down the hall, pausing at Tommy's room: two twin beds with wooden headboards, bookshelves laden with trophies from every conceivable sport, his baseball card collection filling up several shoe boxes, my cheerleading picture in a clear plastic frame.

His bedroom looked different tonight, though. Last night our cheer squad had come over and decorated the room with "Falcon Spirit." It was a Falcons cheerleaders' tradition. We'd put up big posters with slogans like Falcons Flying High Tonight!, Tommy's name, and 43 drawn on them in funky cartoon-style lettering. We'd draped blue-and-white streamers from the ceiling. I'd baked several dozen chocolate chip cookies, and we'd stuck them in a huge metal tin filled with Nestlé's Crunch chocolates, jelly beans, and a Powerbar or two. Mr. and Mrs. Jansen were our coconspirators: We knew that Tommy was going over to Tim Rice's house. The Jansens let us in, and we went wild. The squad did this for every starting player at least once in the season.

I sat down on Tommy's bed and helped myself to one of my cookies. There were just a few left. Tommy had thanked me, along with the rest of the cheerleaders, today at school. He'd seemed truly appreciative and all, but . . . but there was something about his reaction that kind of bothered me. If someone had gone to so much trouble for me, I would have been falling all over myself with gratitude. But Tommy just took it in stride, as if being made a fuss over was all in a day's work. My efforts weren't noticed more than any of the other girls'.

I guessed that was how it was when you were a star on the football team. People treated you like a king, and you lapped it up. A person would have to be crazy not to, I supposed. And if anybody was a king at Fletcher High, it was Tommy. I looked out the window, wondering how long it would be until he returned.

A pair of headlights flashed in the driveway, shooting a beam of light on the photograph of me. I smiled to myself, thinking of how the girls last night had thought it was so romantic of Tommy to keep my picture on his nightstand.

If anyone had told me back in May that I'd be in his bedroom, eating his cookies, hugging his pillow, and looking at a picture of myself staring back at me, I would have fainted from shock.

Having a boyfriend who was a star like Tommy wasn't easy. But it was definitely worth it.

Wasn't it?

Tommy and Lance returned, having had no luck at the Marketplace or at two other stores they'd tried. Tommy and I had put on our coats and were huddled out on the back patio, trying to convince ourselves that summer wasn't over yet. "This sucks," Tommy said.

I shrugged, content with the Sprite I'd found in the Jansens' refrigerator. "I don't think so," I told him truthfully. "We're together."

Tommy put his arms around me. "That's right," he said, grazing my forehead with his lips. "I'm a pretty lucky guy, aren't I?"

I sighed at his words, savoring the feel of his arms. Finally, after what seemed like forever, we were alone.

As if he were reading my mind, Tommy tilted my chin up to meet his. "You don't think you could call your parents and tell them you're spending the night at Holland's, do you?" Tommy asked, only half joking.

"No way! She left right after the game for a choral competition tomorrow with her singing group in North Carolina. My parents know all about it."

Tommy moved his hands up my back. "That's too bad."

We began to kiss out there on his patio. It was the way I'd imagined it would be, away from the crowds at the football game, away from his well-meaning but sports-obsessed buddies, away from the eyes of all the girls I knew were jealous of me and Tommy. . . .

"Yo, Jansen!" Randy Choi pulled open the sliding glass doors and burst out on the patio. "Hey, sorry, Shauna. But Jansen, you've got to see this. ESPN's doing a show on great linebackers of all time, and they're gonna do something on Kevin Greene! He's going to talk about some of the tricks he uses to read a running back's moves in the backfield."

"Oh, man, I've gotta see that!" Tommy said, his face lighting up. "I'll be right in." He turned to me. "You were getting cold out here anyway, weren't you?"

I shrugged. "Not really." I looked down at the ceramic patio tiles beneath my feet. "I just wish for one minute you could stop talking about football," I said slowly. *And that your friends could let us have a moment alone.*

Tommy shot me a surprised look. "This won't take forever, Shaw. And it sounds really cool. I could pick up some great tips from him." He tweaked my nose. "Don't you know how important this kind of thing is to me?"

"Sure I do," I backtracked. "I know it's important. We'll go in," I said, pushing my needs aside and slipping through the glass doors. "You don't want to miss anything."

An hour later Tommy killed the ignition in the Blazer and loosened his seat belt. It had become our ritual . . . Tommy driving me home, parking halfway down the block from my house, making out. But this night, as much as I'd wanted to be with him earlier, right at that moment all I wanted was to go inside and crawl in my bed. My heavy school load along with the physical exertion of cheering in the fresh air had me completely exhausted.

I laid my hand on his arm. "Tommy, I'm beat. I really just want to go to sleep."

Tommy looked puzzled. "I thought you wanted to be alone with me."

"I did, but I guess I'm more tired than I thought."

Tommy gazed out the window. "We lose the game. Then we can't get beer. And now you don't even want to sit here with me for a few minutes?" He heaved a sigh. "Some night."

"No, no, Tommy, it's not that I don't," I said, little prickles of anxiety tickling my neck. "I've just had a hard week. School, cheerleading. I've got a lot to handle. You know I've got this killer math exam coming up—"

Tommy put his finger on my lips, shushing me. "It's okay, Shaw. You don't have to talk me into it." He started the car and slowly drove the rest of the way down the block to my house. "I'll call you tomorrow."

When we reached my driveway, I leaned over for a quick kiss. "Good night," I whispered.

"Do you want me to walk you up?" Tommy asked as we pulled apart.

"Nah. I'll be okay." I took my things and slid out of the Blazer, quietly shutting the car door behind me.

I'd been so excited that afternoon, anticipating being with Tommy after the game, but a feeling of gloom had now overcome me. There were some things about Tommy that were beginning to bother me . . . things I hadn't picked up on when I'd been an admirer-at-large. Every time I wanted to tell Tommy something, something that was important in my life, the conversation always seemed to swing back to him. He *acted* interested in me, but I was starting to notice that he never really listened to what I said. My thoughts flickered back to Brain Drain. Chad never missed a syllable when I spoke.

I sighed. Maybe I was being ridiculous. After all, Chad was my tutor. He was being paid to listen to me. And it wasn't like Tommy and I weren't having any fun. Not only did I like being with him, his kisses were great and I was the envy of all the cheerleaders. So he didn't hang on my every word. Was that such a problem?

My parents had left the outside porch light on, and I stood under it, temporarily blinded by its brightness, and watched as Tommy sped off down the street, his stereo cranked as high as it would go.

As I fumbled with the key in the lock and opened the door I pushed an unwelcome thought out of my brain. A thought I didn't want to let myself think.

That maybe the porch light wasn't the only light that had been blinding me these days.

Eight

Chad

SHAUNA SIGHED. "I give up. I can't do this anymore!" She put her head down on the carrel. "This is driving me crazy!" she said, her voice muffled.

It was more than a week since the football game at Jefferson. If Shauna had noticed my nervousness that night, she hadn't mentioned it, and for that I was grateful. We'd settled into a pretty regular routine of homework and work sheets, and I'd even thrown her a few curveballs by springing an occasional pop quiz. This math exam she had coming up was really important. If she didn't do well on it, she could kiss her passing average good-bye.

"Just write one more biconditional form?" I coaxed.

"No!"

I could see that we'd reached the point of no return: pupil rebellion. There was nothing more I could say or do this Monday afternoon that would motivate Shauna into learning. She was fed up . . . and full of resistance. I realized it was time to get creative.

I handed Shauna her sweater and grabbed my jacket. "Come on. I want to show you something."

She lifted her head. "Something outside?" she asked, looking at the outstretched sweater, her eyes puzzled.

"Just come on."

Behind Fletcher High there was a well-worn dirt path that followed along a grassy incline. Sloping slightly upward, it flattened out into a wide expanse of grass. A small grove of oak trees clustered there, their branches providing welcome shade on a sunny afternoon or cool shadows on a slightly overcast day like today. I often came here after putting in my time at Brain Drain. The grove was a good place to think, and I liked how the hard, knotted roots of the oaks curled under my back when I rested against them.

I sat down underneath one of the trees and patted the grass beside me. "Sit down."

"Why'd you bring me out here?" she asked, looking around her as if I'd hidden some surprise behind one of the trees. She tapped the ground with a tentative motion. "Good thing I'm wearing jeans. The ground feels a little springy."

"Shhh." I motioned for her to be quiet. "It's fine. Just relax." I leaned back on my elbows and closed my eyes partway.

Reluctantly she complied. "This is supposed to

help me do better on my math homework?" she asked after a moment.

"It might," I answered mysteriously. Neither one of us said anything for a few minutes. In the distance I could see the cross-country team making its way around the track, little clouds of dust trailing in its wake. A couple of girls on bicycles came pedaling up the path and coasted past us, their voices lost in the wind. An elderly man walked by with a tiny white poodle on a chain, pulling and tugging this way and that.

"So are you going to keep me in suspense or what?" Shauna finally blurted.

I opened one eye and gestured behind me. "Take a look at the trees. See anything unusual about them?"

Shauna twisted her neck around. "No, not really. Standard oaks."

"No, come on," I persisted. "It's right in front of your face."

She looked at them again. "Um, well, they're covered with kudzu," she said tentatively. "Is that it?"

"Yes," I said, sitting up. "Precisely."

Shauna rolled her eyes, exasperated. "That's not exactly newsworthy, Chad."

Kudzu was a leafy green vine that had set up shop in the South. Everything from telephone poles to porches to trees was potential kudzu territory.

"Yeah, I know you know what kudzu is, but do you know about it? How it grows?"

She shrugged. "Not really."

"Years ago people planted it because they

thought it was pretty." I lowered my voice. "That was before they learned about the terrible dark secret of . . . kudzu."

Shauna giggled. "And what, pray tell, is so dark and terrible about kudzu?"

I raised my eyebrows. "You scoff, do you? Well, on those horrible, stinking hot, humid days we have in the summer, the kudzu vine can grow up to a foot."

Shauna gasped. "In one day?"

"In one day."

Shauna reached over and gave the vine a firm, verifying yank. "That's so weird! Like something in a science fiction story. Growing that much in one day doesn't seem normal."

I grinned. She'd walked right into my trap. "That's exactly my point. It's not normal. And neither would you be if you picked up all the math principles that I'm trying to teach you in one day or one week. Even two weeks."

"So that's what this is about." Shauna's mouth twisted into a wry smile.

"Yep." Impulsively I took her hand. "Shauna, you're doing really well."

"Yeah, right," she said, her tone disdainful. But I noticed she was looking at me, waiting to hear what I was going to say next.

"So you don't understand everything. Just keep at it. If you stay dedicated and try to be enthusiastic, you're going to do well. I know it." I squeezed her hand.

"I hope you're right," she said quietly.

We sat like that for several minutes, breathing in the kudzu's grapey scent, the sun making an appearance to warm our cheeks. My hand had returned to my lap. I'd been so dazed with myself for touching her in the first place that both myself and my hand had been momentarily paralyzed.

The school, a little glass prism in the distance, sparkled in the sleepy afternoon light. It was getting late.

Reluctantly I stood up, brushing some twigs and dirt off my jeans. "We should head back inside. You probably have to get going."

Shauna squinted up at me. "Chad?"

"Yes?"

"I know our session for today is technically over, but if you don't mind, I was thinking maybe we could go over that last chapter again. I feel much fresher now."

"Sure. Sure, we can," I said, grinning at her. "We've got all the time you want."

Unfortunately that wasn't exactly true.

After our visit to the oak grove we returned to Brain Drain and put our noses to the grindstone. Page after page I went over Shauna's homework assignments for the week, making sure she grasped every concept before moving on to the next one.

"If you don't understand something, you've got to stop because math is built on a foundation," I instructed. "If it's not solid in your brain, you'll never fully get what's coming around the bend."

We sat there for another hour working and reworking the problems in her textbook until the janitor tapped on the glass at the entrance. He pointed to his watch. "Time to go, kids," he mouthed.

I nodded. "I hear you."

"Too bad we have to quit," I said to Shauna. "You were really on a roll."

Shauna looked thoughtful. "We don't have to quit. If you want to come over, we could study at my house. I'm sure my parents would pay you extra."

"Well, um, that's not necessary," I said, glad that she wasn't ready to end our afternoon just yet. I knew it was just a tutoring session, but I was really having fun being with her. "That wouldn't be right. I didn't have any plans tonight anyway," I told her truthfully. *Great. Could I make myself sound a little more available?*

"Okay. Well, good. But if you're coming over to tutor me for free, then I'm going to be forced to feed you dinner."

I grabbed my stomach. "If you must, I'm your willing eater."

"Are you Shauna's boyfriend?" asked the little blonde who was in-line skating in front of Shauna's house. Shauna and I were sitting on the steps of her crumbling brick porch, underneath a canopy of silvery green Spanish moss.

"I'm afraid not," I said, crouching down to her level. I really liked kids. I didn't have any brothers or sisters, and I'd always thought I'd missed out on something there.

Shauna pursed her lips. "Amber, I want you and

96

Lindsey to play in the garage. You can skate in there."

Amber looked from Lindsey to Shauna, clearly uncertain as to who held the upper hand.

"But we like skating on the sidewalk in front of the house!" Lindsey, a miniature version of Shauna, protested.

"Well, you're bugging us. We can't study if you keep skating by and asking silly questions."

Lindsey pouted. "You're not being fair."

Amber zipped past us, her arms flailing wildly. "Yeah, Shauna. You're not being fair." Then she looked at me. "If you're not Shauna's boyfriend, you could be mine."

I was seriously considering the offer when Shauna stood up. "We'd better go inside," she muttered. "We'll never get any work done with these pests out here."

"Pests? Nah. I think they're kind of cute," I declared, following Shauna in the house. I actually welcomed the distraction because I was having a tough time keeping my eyes off Shauna. Jamie was right—she *was* gorgeous.

"If you lived with one of them, you'd change your tune in a hurry, mister."

I'd never tutored anyone outside Brain Drain before. The Phillipses' house was similar in layout to mine, except it was a little messier. We set up our stuff in the family room, and I called my folks to let them know where I was. Shauna's mother brought us a tray of diced carrots and celery and some iced tea. "Now don't spoil your appetite," she cautioned. "You're in luck, Chad. I'm making one of Shauna's favorites tonight. Chicken barbecue and potatoes au gratin."

Shauna patted her stomach appreciatively. "Don't tempt me, Mom," she said, smiling over at me. "I'm totally starving right now."

I smiled too and risked one more look at Shauna. Mrs. Phillips was right. I really was in luck tonight.

Dinner was great, and afterward Shauna helped her mom clean up the kitchen while Lindsey and I watched *Wheel of Fortune*. I'd tried to help, but Mrs. Phillips had shooed me out of the way. "You're our guest, Chad. Please."

"I like you," Lindsey said during a commercial break.

"I like you too," I told her.

She frowned. "I don't like Shauna's boyfriend."

"Why not?" I asked, not being able to help my curiosity.

Lindsey crossed her arms. "He ran over one of my Barbies with his car. It was one of my favorites too."

I tried to suppress a grin. "I'm sure he didn't mean it."

Lindsey didn't look too sure about that.

"So is she talking your ear off or what?" Shauna said, walking into the room. I smiled up at her. Unfortunately she'd changed out of the flirty thigh-revealing dress she'd had on in school into a pair of green denim cutoffs and an oversize sweatshirt that read If Cheerleading Were Easy, It'd Be Called Football.

"Nice shirt," I said, laughing.

"Holland got them for us." Shauna sat down on the floor across from me and began doing leg lifts. "We only wear them at home, though. They could start trouble at school."

"Yeah, I can think of a few guys who wouldn't be too amused," I said dryly.

After *Wheel* we watched *Jeopardy*. "This must be required viewing for Brain Drainers," Shauna teased. Now she was in the middle of some complicated stretch move, her chin flush with the floor.

I groaned good-naturedly. "Come on. We're not as brainy as all that. Are we?" I decided to keep the fact that my father was once a contestant—and that if they ever had tryouts in South Carolina for *Teen Jeopardy* I'd be the first in line—to myself.

Shauna shook her head. "No, funny enough, you're not." She sat up and curled her feet under her Indian style. For a moment we locked eyes with each other, and something in my stomach flip-flopped ever so slightly.

"What Amber asked you before—outside—about you having a girlfriend. Do you?" she asked. "I mean, we've spent a lot of time together, and I realized I didn't know that about you."

"No. I don't," I answered, surprised that she'd even be interested. "I haven't had a lot of free time."

"I know what you mean," Shauna agreed. "This is the first night in days that I've sat down and let myself watch TV. It's kind of nice to let your mind focus on something perfectly mindless."

"But you weren't exactly sitting. And this isn't exactly mindless," I pointed out. "It's all about numbers, really. Especially in Double Jeopardy."

Shauna made a face. "You're right. We must be able to find something more mind numbing to do."

I laughed, stretching out my arms behind my head. "So what would you be doing right now if I weren't here?" I asked.

"Looking in the mirror and rubbing cream on her face," Lindsey blurted. "That's what she was doing last night." Lindsey pretended to slather some invisible cream on her cheeks, forehead, and oddly enough, her head.

"That is *it!*" Shauna declared, going over to the rocking chair where Lindsey sat and giving it a playful shove. "You are the clear winner of the most embarrassing younger sibling of the year award."

"Huh?" Lindsey said, baffled.

"Come on," Shauna said suddenly, dragging Lindsey up from the couch and motioning for me to follow along behind her. "I've got the perfect couch potato antidote."

"You're winning, Chad, you're winning!" Lindsey clapped gleefully from the sidelines.

"Thank you, thank you." I took a bow. "But may I remind you, young lady, you are the official referee here tonight. That means you've got to stay impartial. You can't want one of us to win more than the other."

"That's right," Shauna spoke up, picking up the shuttlecock and smacking it firmly over the clothes-line that served as a makeshift badminton net. The patio behind me was one boundary, the thick bushy hedge behind Shauna was the other; we'd left the side perimeters open.

"Well, I want Chad to win," Lindsey whined, sticking her tongue out at Shauna.

We battled back and forth for several minutes. "You play pretty well," I gasped, lunging for the birdie. "But I play better." With a whack I sent the shuttlecock flying, embedding it deep into the boundary hedge. "Oops, sorry. I'll get it," I offered. I jogged over and reached my arms down among the densely packed branches.

The back screen door opened. "Shauna?" Mrs. Phillips waved to us. "Tommy's on the phone. Give this to Shauna," she instructed Lindsey, handing her the cordless.

Lindsey scowled at the phone before walking over and handing it to her sister.

Successfully retrieving the birdie, I pulled out my arms. They were covered with little red, painful scratches.

"Hello?" Shauna paused. A slow red flush began to spread over her cheeks. "Do I?" She laughed nervously. "I'm outside, fooling around with Lindsey. Yeah. Yeah, I know." She looked over at me, and I sensed that she was feeling uncomfortable.

"Hey, Lindsey, how about showing me that bicycle trick you were telling me about earlier?" I asked softly.

"Okay!" she said brightly, running toward the garage.

I started to follow her. "No! Wait right here!" she commanded.

"Hold on a minute, Tommy." Shauna put her hand over the mouthpiece. "I'll only be a few minutes."

"Don't worry about it." I stood there awkwardly, trying to appear extremely attentive to the large metal bug zapper that sizzled every few seconds. Pretending you aren't listening to a conversation you're dying to hear is a hard thing to do.

I wondered why Shauna hadn't mentioned that I was there too. Would Tommy get mad if he knew?

Lindsey came back empty-handed, her mouth drawn down into a pout. "Mom said I can't show you the trick. I have to go in and have my bath."

I patted her little concave shoulder. "Maybe another time," I consoled.

Her eyes lit up. "Are you going to come over again?" she asked as she trudged into the house.

I hesitated. "Uh, maybe. I'll have to see about that."

Just then Shauna clicked off. When we were playing the game, her cheeks had been flushed full of excitement, her expression happy and carefree. Now she looked tired, and little dots of worry flickered in her eyes.

"Sorry about that," Shauna apologized.

"Is everything okay?" I asked. "You look upset."

Shauna swatted at a mosquito on her leg. "No. I'm fine."

I looked at my watch. "Listen, I should really be going. It's getting late, and I did have some stuff I wanted to finish up at home."

Her face fell. "Are you sure you can't stay? I was thinking that maybe I could make some popcorn. . . ." She drifted off.

"I wish I could," I said regretfully, handing her the badminton equipment. "I've got some things to do, though. Maybe another time. And besides," I kidded, "I know a girl who has some math homework to do."

Shauna sighed. "Funny, I know that girl too. I guess I'll see you in school tomorrow, then. Thanks a lot for the extra help tonight, Chad."

"Anytime. Tell your mom how much I enjoyed the barbecue. It was great."

"I will."

The air felt thick and moist as I walked to my car. I bent down to tie my shoe, and when I stood up, Shauna had gone into the house. From my vantage point on the lawn I could see Shauna through the window as she opened up the refrigerator and poured herself a glass of juice. Wiping her lips with her hand, she leaned against the kitchen doorway, her head tilted back, her eyes almost closed, as if she was dreaming.

Shauna looked so beautiful. I felt slightly weak at the sight of her.

Wistfully I crept through the damp night grass to my car, a smart but lonely boy in the night.

Nine

Shauna

"SO DOES EVERYONE have their lollipop bags?" Erica Terry asked at the end of practice, her gaze roving from one girl to the next.

Our squad was trying to come up with money to fund the decorating and food purchases we made for "Falcons Spirit," as well as start a fund for cheer camp next summer. We had planned several small fund-raisers to take place throughout the year, the first being the Lollipop Blast—selling multiflavored pops for fifty cents apiece.

"We can earn more than fifty percent profit. And the weeks before Halloween have always been a great time to fund-raise." Erica shook a lollipop at us. "Just make sure you keep the pops with you . . . and out of your locker. Last year we had to dump several bags of lollipops that had been stored in lockers—they melted."

We all nodded in empathy. Our school was

famous for the heat ducts that passed behind the lockers. Sometimes the lockers got so warm, you could almost fry a hamburger in them.

"I really liked that new cheer we learned today," I told Holland as we headed into the locker room to change.

"Yeah. It had definite attitude." She opened her locker. "You want to go to the mall with Claire and me?" she asked, pulling her snug black turtleneck over her head. "We're pretty psyched. Claire heard they're having a mallwide sidewalk sale. Her older sister's taking us."

Shopping was always tempting, but not today. "I can't. I've got to redo my math proofs from last night. I got two wrong, and Chad always asks me to do the ones I missed again until I get them right. And I've got to keep studying for the math test."

Holland closed her eyes and brushed some pale beige shadow over her lids. "That new cheer isn't the only thing that's got attitude around here. You do too. A new one."

"Passing math's the only way I can stay on the squad and keep seeing Tommy," I pointed out.

Holland bent down to pull on a clean pair of socks. "And it seems that getting there has been half the fun."

Holland's remark stopped me mid-lip-gloss application.

Because she had a point.

I practically skipped out of the library after my Wednesday session with Chad. Things were going better than I could have expected—I had gotten so many things right that I'd only had to use my eraser twice!

Normally the halls were pretty much deserted at this time of day, so I was startled to see Tommy and Lance rounding the corner.

"Hi!" I greeted them, surprised.

"Football practice was cut short today. Partly because of the heat and partly because Coach wants us to rest up for Friday's game," Tommy explained.

I raised my eyebrows. "Sounds like Prescott's getting soft."

Tommy slung his arm around my shoulders. "So we definitely should take advantage of the situation, don't you think?"

"Definitely," I agreed.

"You want to come over and go swimming?" Tommy asked. "The pool's still pretty warm."

"Sure," I said, beaming at him. It would be so nice to have some one-on-one time—

"You too, Lance. Anybody else you want to call?"

Lance grinned. "Oh, I can think of a few people."

"We'll swing by your house and you can grab your suit, Shauna."

"Great," I said, forcing a cheery smile to my lips. The more the merrier.

"This was such a good idea," Chrissy said, leaning over me to grab the suntan lotion. This was her third—or was it fourth?—application in less than an hour. And the sun was practically setting.

"Yeah," I said halfheartedly, looking around me. What had started out as an intimate gathering of me, Tommy, and Lance had turned into a dozen of Tommy's closest friends having an end-of-Indian-summer poolside bash. Chrissy and John, Randy and Joy, Falcon juniors Bill, Tim, and Shane, and a bunch of girls from the cheerleading squad were all there.

A wicked game of volleyball was taking place in the Jansens' pool—definitely too much testosterone in that match for me to get involved.

"So I guess we're the designated scorekeepers," I said to Joy.

"Yeah." She pulled self-consciously at her white bikini top. "There's no way I'm jumping around in there with this on."

I nodded. You'd think after years of going to the beach that I'd feel comfortable in a bikini by now, but I wasn't. I'd put on the cutest one I owned: lavender and pink checks, with little daisy bra straps. But still, all this flesh made me a little shy.

Suddenly the volleyball whizzed up and hit my beach chair. "Why don't you join us?" Tommy called, swimming over to the pool's edge, his hands outstretched to retrieve the ball.

"And miss all this juicy girl talk?" I replied as I tossed the ball back to him.

Tommy caught the ball and flipped it to Randy. Then he hoisted himself out of the pool and came over to me. "It's no fun having you over here while I'm in there," he whispered in my ear.

I shivered as water droplets slid off Tommy's muscular body and onto me. "Likewise."

Tommy crouched down, his hair a mass of soft, wet waves. "Then come in."

"I don't want to play volleyball."

"You don't have to."

Just then a roar went up from the pool. Natalie Smith had dived in, taking Tommy's place on the informal volleyball team.

"See, Natalie's not afraid to play with the boys," Tommy said. I couldn't help but notice the admiring glance he gave her and her slick red bikini.

"I'm not afraid," I responded tartly.

"Then come in," Tommy urged, giving my chair a little pull.

"I told you—I don't want to."

"So why'd you come over?" Tommy asked.

I shook my head at his apparent mental block. "To be with you."

Tommy poked my toe with his. "But you are."

"Could have fooled me," I said, unable to hold my resentment back. The ironic thing was, Tommy had been complaining all week that I couldn't hang out as much and that I was cutting our phone conversations short.

"It has nothing to do with you," I'd protest, trying to soothe his wounded ego while not admitting that he was right. "Do you think I like studying all the time?"

"No," he'd say grudgingly.

"Well, if I don't, I'm going to be in serious trouble."

We'd kiss and make up, and I'd blame our problems on the fact that we were a new couple, still getting used to each other's rhythms.

But I was afraid there was more to it than that.

I slipped on my sandals, not bothering to wait for his reply. "I'm going home," I said petulantly.

Tommy put his hands on my shoulders. "Shauna, you're being crazy. What's wrong?"

I looked away, my eyes threatening to spill tears at any moment.

"Aw, come on, Shauna," Tommy said. He took my hand and squeezed it. "Come inside with me. We'll get something to drink, okay?"

I nodded.

Inside the kitchen Tommy opened the fridge and handed me an ice-cold can of Coke. "I thought you were having a good time," he said, his tone one of confusion.

"I am." I wrapped my arms around myself and wished I'd grabbed my T-shirt. "I just would like to spend more time alone with you."

Tommy cracked open his own can of soda. "You don't like my friends?"

"It's not that," I protested. "It's that I like *you*." *Or at least I want to,* I thought miserably. But I was beginning to learn that liking Tommy from afar and being in a relationship with him were two very different things. Things I hadn't counted on before we met.

Tommy sat down on one of the barstools that surrounded the extended countertop and pulled me between his legs.

"You're dripping all over," I told him.

"Forget about that." Tommy kissed my forehead. "I want things to work out for us, Shauna. I like you a lot. But I can't give up my friends for you."

"I'm not asking you to," I said softly. "But you have to give me something."

Tommy put his arms around me, which was a good thing because my knees were beginning to quiver. "What's that?"

"A couple hours a week."

Tommy leaned forward and hugged me. "I'll do my best."

I closed my eyes and buried my face in his neck. I couldn't ask him to do anything more.

On Friday night the Falcons won their home game 28–21, and as usual we cheerleaders stood outside the Falcons locker room, waiting to cheer the guys on. Tommy looked extra handsome tonight: The past few days he'd spent outdoors had made his light hair look even more sun kissed than usual. And he was in his element, having gained yardage left and right and being the one player the Falcons could always rely on.

I was embarrassed over the way I had acted the other day—like a spoiled brat. I vowed I would be stronger from now on. Tommy's popularity had intrigued me for months. Giving him grief over it would be a total turnoff.

"Shauna! Holland! Over here!" I turned at the sound of my mother's voice. She gestured toward the parking lot. "Lindsey and I will wait for you

110

two in the car," she called. "Don't be long!"

I gave her the thumbs–up sign. Mark, Holland's official boyfriend now, had gone to visit colleges that weekend, and Holland and I had made plans to hang out that night.

Tommy spotted me right away when he came out of the locker room. He grinned and held up his finger, as if to say, "Just one minute."

I waved back, watching as Tommy joked with some of his teammates. Then the coach and his assistant pulled him aside for a few minutes of heavy conversation. Then it was back to the guys again. Five minutes went by. Ten. Fifteen. I was starting to get steamed. "He knows my mom is waiting for us," I complained to Holland.

She shrugged and jiggled from foot to foot. "I'd give him two more minutes, max."

"You mean just leave?" I said, slightly horrified at the idea.

"Unless you're one of his groupies, yeah."

Finally he broke away from the jock clique . . . and began flirting with some of the junior varsity cheerleaders, who were falling all over him.

I heard my mom's horn beep.

"C'mon," I said, spinning on my heel. "We've waited long enough." I pushed my way through the throng before Tommy could see that I was gone.

If he even bothered to look.

"You two looked terrific out there," my mom said as we cruised along the highway. She was really

111

good about attending my games. My dad usually had to be at the hotel on Friday nights, so my mom and Lindsey had a mother-daughter thing going on. That night my mom had taken Lindsey out to dinner and then they came to the game. Feeding Lindsey before the game was a smart move because that way she was too full to pester my mom for the concession stand junk food.

"Thanks," Holland and I said in unison. My mom was listening to our favorite radio station. She always did that when I had friends in the car. I think she was trying to impress them by showing how hip she still was.

"Guess who we saw tonight?" Lindsey asked, turning around from her shotgun seat.

"Tommy," I replied, already feeling guilty for striding away from him without saying anything.

"Nope," she said, delighted to have something on me. "Try again."

"Bubba Red," Holland offered. We all laughed. Bubba Red was this corny guy in a clown outfit who did commercials for a local South Carolina bank. His famous line was, "Bank right—it's a deeee-light!"

"No." Lindsey folded her arms across her chest. "We saw Chad."

I leaned forward. "Chad Givens?"

"He came over and sat with us for part of the game," my mom informed us. "I really like him, Shauna. He's so polite."

"Was he there alone?" I asked, my curiosity piqued.

"He was there with a group of people," Lindsey said helpfully.

"A group of guys?" Holland prodded.

"Guys and girls," my mom said. At the next red light she stopped and turned to look at us. "Do I detect some interest back here?"

"Get real, Mom," I huffed, settling back in my seat. "We've both got boyfriends."

"Then I guess it wouldn't matter that he was with a striking-looking brunette," my mom said casually.

"He what?" I gasped.

My mom's chirpy laughter came from the front seat. "Not to worry; that last part's not true. Just a little test."

As Holland broke into peals of laughter I clamped my mouth shut, refusing to take any more bait. I'd forgotten a cardinal rule. Never trust a mother who likes the same music you do.

Holland and I hadn't spent the night together since school started, and I was suffering from major sleep-over withdrawal. Before we reached my house, my mom stopped at the shopping center so that we could pick up some Krispy Kreme doughnuts for breakfast the next morning and a couple of movies at Blockbuster: *My Best Friend's Wedding* for Holland (she said she wanted something completely sappy and romantic) and for me, *Gone with the Wind* (the whole Scarlett-Ashley-Rhett thing always intrigued me).

We only made it through a few of Julia Roberts's dazzling smiles, though, before we were all practically falling asleep. Leaving my mom curled up on the couch, Holland and I dragged ourselves down the hall to my room. Inside my bathroom I sat down on the side of the tub and watched as Holland began to take off her eye makeup.

"So," she said, dabbing her lids with oil-free remover. "What exactly's going on with you and Tommy?"

I sighed dejectedly. "I don't know." Ever since the pool party at his house on Wednesday afternoon, I hadn't known how I felt or what to think.

"He's going to be angry that I left without saying good-bye," I mumbled.

"He'll get over it." She splashed her face with cold water, patting it dry with one of my big fluffy bath towels. "The pool party didn't sound that awful, you know."

I hugged my knees to my chest, stretching my favorite old blue cotton nightshirt to its limits. "No, I guess it wasn't." I shrugged and picked up my body scrub sponge. "You know, Hol," I said, absently tossing the sponge in the air, "I wanted Tommy for so long."

"I know."

"But now I . . . he . . ." I trailed off.

"Now that the chase is over, it's no fun anymore," Holland pronounced.

"That's not it," I objected. I put the sponge back on the edge of the tub. "There are so many things I like about him: his confident attitude, his killer looks, his amazing body. . . ."

"Maybe that's the problem," Holland suggested

as we went back into my room. "You liked him before you ever knew what he really was about. Before you got the chance to know the person inside behind the beautiful face."

I thought about that as I turned off my lamp and we crawled into my bed. Maybe Holland was right. Maybe that was all that hooked me. The superficial stuff. I buried my face in my pillow.

"And what's up with Chad?"

For some reason I could feel my cheeks turn a maddening shade of red. "Well, you know, I'm there three days a week, and—"

"Duh. No. I mean, what's up romantically?"

I hit her with a spare pillow. "Holland, in case you missed it, we're just friends."

"Nothing more?" she prodded.

"No," I insisted. I let out a sigh. "I mean, I guess it would be cool if Tommy could be a little more like Chad in certain ways," I said thoughtfully, flipping over on my back. "But don't get me wrong, I don't like *Chad*," I added hastily. "It's just that he's so sweet. He's nice, you know?"

"Maybe rather than trying to change the person you're with *into* someone else, you should just change the person *for* someone else," Holland said softly.

There wasn't much I could say to that. I lay on my back, staring up at the Day-Glo stars that were stuck to the ceiling above my head. They formed an outline of the Big Dipper. My dad and I had put them up there when I was in sixth grade, but they'd still retained their glow after all these years. I'd been fascinated by the solar system, and my parents had gotten me this colorful mobile and hundreds of ceiling stickers. For my birthday that year they'd sent away to some astronomy organization and "bought" me a star. I'd never heard of something so cool, and for a long time I'd stared out my window for hours every night, trying to make out my own star in the sky.

When I was younger, I used to look up to the stars whenever I had a problem and try to find the answer spelled out somehow. And somehow there always was one, waiting.

Making sure I didn't wake Holland, who was now snoring lightly, I tiptoed out of my bed and walked over to the window. A cool breeze slightly ruffled my blinds as I lifted them. I stared out into the inky black darkness.

There weren't any stars in the sky tonight.

I leaned my head against the window frame. Despite their absence I knew there was an answer waiting for me. An answer that would tell me what to do with my life.

If only I could find it.

Ten

Chad

*C*HECK. CHECK. CHECK. I went down the list of answers Shauna had provided on the latest set of work sheets I'd given her. She sat beside me, her spine straight and her hands folded on her lap.

"I'm afraid there's a problem here," I told her sternly.

"There is?" she asked, her voice small.

"Yes. You're a Brain Drain pupil, but you've turned in three perfect papers. We're going to have to do something about that."

"Yes!" Shauna yelled, making a fist and pumping her arm. Then she giggled. "I guess I'm not supposed to do that in here, am I?" she whispered, grinning. "It's just that I'm so excited! I'm actually understanding this stuff!"

"This is cause for celebration," I said, pulling her to her feet. "Ever been to Broadway?"

*　　*　　*

"Chad, this was an incredible idea," Shauna enthused as we exited from Ben & Jerry's, each of us holding a gigantic waffle cone. I'd brought her to Broadway at the Beach, one of the biggest and most popular shopping and entertainment centers in South Carolina, about ten minutes from where we lived. After debating on whether to hit Planet Hollywood or the pyramid-shaped Hard Rock Café and deciding we were a little short on cash to do either, we'd both agreed that a simple cone would really hit the spot.

I took a big lick of vanilla fudge. "Don't think I'm doing this for fun," I said, trying to sound strict. "It's all based on mathematics, really."

"And how's that?"

I held out the ice-cream cone. "Well, this ice-cream cone, for example. You made it perfectly clear that you wanted two scoops, not one. If it weren't for math, the ice cream guy would have had no idea what you meant."

"Why, I'd never thought of it that way," Shauna said dramatically, going along with me. "Just think if we didn't have numbers. We might have to walk around with gallons of ice cream on our cones!"

A Korean couple walked by, pushing a baby carriage. They were talking to their baby in Korean. I strained to make out the words.

"Do you know them?" Shauna asked.

"No." I told her about my tae kwon do class. "We had to learn some basic Korean words, or else we'd never be able to understand what Master

Chung wants us to do. It's fun to see if I can actually decipher a conversation."

We strolled along, our faces dappled by the autumn sunlight. October was a beautiful month in Myrtle Beach. Even the air had a different scent to it. The aromas of suntan oil and Sunday barbecues were gone, replaced with a tinge of oak leaves and pumpkin patches.

There were several large pedestrian bridges at Broadway at the Beach, each crossing over huge expanses of a man-made lake. We stopped, leaning against one of the railings and looking at all the funky, colorful restaurants that lined the waterside.

"So what's it like, walking around with a genius IQ?" Shauna asked.

"I don't know any other way," I teased. "I've been a boy genius all my life." I leaned back, letting the sun hit me full on in the face. "No, seriously. I don't even know what my IQ is. Probably the same as yours. I just like math . . . and as a result I've always done well."

Shauna bit into her cone. "I used to like math until *Connected Mathematics* came along. And then I started hating it." She smiled up at me. "But you made me like math again, Chad. You made it fun."

I smiled back. "I'm glad."

We walked along the bridge, stopping at a glass box filled with some kind of fish food. "Do you have a quarter?" I asked, fumbling around in my pocket.

"Are you kidding?" She snapped open a tiny leather change purse and forked over several. "I've got a million of them, courtesy of the Lollipop Blast. Lollipops are sure popular."

I stuck a quarter in the slot and turned the handle. A pile of seed fell out.

"What are you going to feed?" she asked, peering down into the murky brown water. "I don't see anything."

"We just have to find the right place. Over here," I called, moving several feet down the bridge. I threw a little food in the water. "Watch."

The waters at Broadway at the Beach were loaded with carp. I don't know if they bred them there or where they came from, but thousands of fish called the place home.

"Chad! Look!" In seconds the place was swarming with the thick, rubbery fish, their pale peach-colored mouths gulping for food.

I flung in the rest of my handful. The carp were now swarming so thick that they swam practically on top of one another, several feet deep. The food disappeared in seconds.

"Here, I'll go get more!" Shauna ran off and returned a few seconds later, her hands cupped to hold several quarters' worth of food. We spent the next few minutes creating a feeding frenzy. The carp drew a lot of attention, and soon we weren't the only ones helping them to get even fatter than they were.

"Wow, that was fun," Shauna said, wiping her hands off on her gray woolen shorts. "Dinnertime isn't easy when you're a carp, I guess."

"That's for sure."

We drifted over to the huge IMAX, the multi-dimensional theater that sat on the edge of the complex. "It's nice this time of year," I mused as we walked. "Now that summer is over, it's finally getting back to normal around here." That was a common complaint among local residents. Tourism was a double-edged sword: The local businesses couldn't survive without the millions of tourist dollars spent here every year, but sometimes you felt like a stranger among a sea of out-of-towners.

"My family doesn't quite feel that way," Shauna confessed. "My dad runs the SeaSpray. Tourists are his life."

"The SeaSpray . . . is that the big pink hotel with the blue ocean mural painted on the side?" I asked, trying to picture it on the Myrtle Beach strip.

Shauna nodded. "I think they're going to paint over the mural this winter, though. It's getting kind of old."

"It must be fun, having your dad run the hotel. Do you ever spend the night there?"

Shauna laughed. "I tried to get my dad to keep an oceanfront suite at my beck and call, but he put the kibosh on that one. He does keep a room free at all times in case he's working late, and then he sleeps over."

I smiled at Shauna as she spoke, admiring the way her wavy hair blew softly in the breeze. I was having a great time. If Shauna didn't have a boyfriend, this would be the point where I'd reach over and take her hand in mine. Even though I hadn't had much experience when it came to girls, and even though Shauna was one of the prettiest and most popular girls at Fletcher, I felt completely at ease with her.

Yes, I daydreamed, *I'd take her beautiful hand, and she'd squeeze mine passionately in return, and we'd spend the rest of the afternoon mooning over each other in giddy ecstasy while sipping piña coladas, and then we'd—*

"Chad? Hello?" Shauna snapped her fingers in front of my face. "You've got the funniest expression! Are you feeling all right?"

"I'm fine," I answered gruffly. I hadn't realized that we'd reached the IMAX already. "Have you ever seen anything here?" I asked quickly, trying to divert attention from my kindled-up cheeks.

"No. You?"

"Yeah. Something about life under the sea. It was really cool." I peered at the list of upcoming movies. "Nothing grabs me now, though."

We ambled back across the bridge and made our way down one of the "streets," stopping to check out some of the tiny boutiques that lined our path. Shauna picked up a bag of gourmet jelly beans for her mom, and I bought a copy of an old John Grisham paperback I'd wanted to read for a long time as well as a really cool ruler that was painted with an underwater coral reef design.

Then, as we passed by a toy store, Shauna's face lit up. "Hey," she said thoughtfully, "there's something in there that I saw last time I was here with my parents and Lindsey. I want to see if they still have it." I started to follow her into the toy store. "Do you mind waiting out here?" she asked, her eyes dancing. "I'll only be a minute."

"Uh, sure." I made myself comfortable on a bench and was just about ready to nod off when Shauna bounced back into view.

"Okay, I'm ready!" she said, clutching a small white paper bag.

"They had what you wanted?" I asked.

She grinned. "Yeah."

We walked down past a row of closed nightclubs. At the end were lots of cement blocks, where various celebrities had left their handprints and signatures. I bent down to get a closer look and to test out my hands in some of the indents.

Suddenly I felt something furry on my face. *"Ki-yop!"* a tiny voice shrieked, sounding like one of the Chipmunks. I spun around, startled.

Shauna stood doubled over with laughter. In her hand was a small stuffed gorilla, dressed in a tae kwon do *dobok*.

"What in the world—" I started.

"It's a Karate Kreature," Shauna wheezed, trying to catch her breath. "I saw these here last time, and after you mentioned that you were interested in the martial arts, I just had to get you one." She pressed the little gorilla's stomach. *"Ahp!"* the gorilla yelped.

"That's what I feel like doing after math class," Shauna declared, laughing.

I grinned back as I took the toy from her. I'd

never had a girl buy me something before. Especially not a girl as amazing as Shauna.

The toy was addictive, and neither of us could stop pressing its tummy. It kept us laughing the entire ride home.

"I really had a good time today, Chad," Shauna said when we reached her house.

"Me too." I meant it. I knew it wasn't a real date. But I couldn't imagine a real date being better than the time Shauna and I had spent together this afternoon. This was by far the best time I had ever had with a girl in my life.

I'd wanted to find the right girl for a while now. And now that I had, how could I make her feel the same way about me?

Eleven

Shauna

CHAD SHUT *CONNECTED Mathematics: Course I* with a resounding slap. "You are ready to kick math butt!" he said, giving me a high five.

"Do you really think so?" I asked nervously. It was the day before the big exam, and we'd just finished going over the suggested review topics Ms. Slater had passed out last week as well as a drill on all the definitions from the first three chapters of the text. I could hardly believe it, but I was actually looking forward to the test. I'd worked so hard for what seemed like so long, and I wanted the chance to strut my stuff in the classroom.

"I know so," Chad declared. "You didn't start out this way, but you have turned out to be one of the most dedicated pupils I've ever had. That Brain Drain's ever had. Maybe all of Horry County's ever had!"

We joked and kidded around for the next few

minutes. I asked Chad a few questions about inductive reasoning just to make sure I was completely ready.

"You're all set," Chad told me. "But I had an idea that I thought might help you. What if we go upstairs to your classroom and sit there for a few minutes?"

"What for?"

"Visualization," Chad declared. "Come on. Let's try it."

The halls were pretty much empty at this time of day, and I could smell the heavy odor of Lysol as the cleaning people swabbed down the floors. Room 211 was locked, but one of the other math teachers who was passing by let us in when we promised to be out in a few minutes.

It felt funny to be in my empty classroom with Chad. The remnants of today's math problems were still on the board, and I felt a warped sense of pride when I pointed out the traces of the problem I had done. "Correctly, of course," I told him.

"Of course." Chad looked around the room. "Now, which seat is yours?" I showed him. "Okay. I want you to sit down and take a few deep breaths."

I did as he said.

"Close your eyes and imagine yourself in class tomorrow. Ms. Slater is passing out the exams and you feel calm, cool, and collected. You're not looking out the window. You're not passing notes. And you're not talking."

"I wouldn't do that!" I protested indignantly, opening my eyes for a flash. Chad had sat down in Billy

Witherspoon's seat, next to me. I decided to keep the fact that Billy had a salivating problem a secret.

"Right. Well, you aren't doing anything but focusing on yourself and what you're about to do," Chad continued. "And then when you open your eyes, the test will be a challenge, not an obstacle."

I pictured myself in class tomorrow as Ms. Slater passed down the tests, row to row. My stomach felt calm. My hands stayed dry. There was nothing she could ask us that I didn't know. I might not get a hundred on it, but I knew there was no way I would fail. A surge of appreciation ran through me. Chad didn't have to be here with me now, helping me to visualize. He was with me out of the goodness of his heart. He was more dedicated to tutoring than some of my teachers were to teaching.

It dawned on me that Holland had suggested I do the same thing back in May, when I'd tried out for cheerleading. I'd been so nervous then, desperate to make cheerleader and snag Tommy in the process. The whole thing seemed so long ago.

When I opened my eyes, Chad was staring at me with a look I couldn't quite read. "I've really enjoyed getting to know you, Shauna," he said quietly, his lips trembling ever so slightly as he spoke.

"Me too," I said, suddenly awkward. I'd been fine during the visualization, but I felt unexpectedly uneasy, as if the room were spinning in circles. What was happening? "I—I think I need to eat something," I said, blaming my queasy stomach on my lack of food today. "Feel like a little pretest celebration and study session at Carlo's pizzeria?"

Chad nodded. "Sure. I've never been there."

"Well, then, there's something *I* can teach *you*." I grinned at him, the awkward moment between us gone. "I'll just have to phone my mom."

"Do you think Tommy will mind?" Chad asked.

"No, not at all," I replied, thinking of him for the first time that afternoon.

My feelings were beginning to frighten me. Because to be honest, I didn't know if I'd care if he did.

After being surrounded by the muggy outside air, it felt good to meet the icy-cold blast of air-conditioning that hit me when I walked into my house.

"Shauna?" my mom called from the backyard, her voice carrying through our screened kitchen windows.

"Yes?"

"Come out here for a minute. I want to talk to you."

I dropped my books on the kitchen counter and went out through the sliding glass doors that led to our patio. As twilight fell, my mom was tending to her rosebushes, which were finally starting to fade away for the season.

"How was your pizza?"

"Great." I'd believed it was possible, but Chad and I had had a great time studying. Over a huge pepperoni pie we'd gone over all the review questions again, and Chad had drilled me for thirty minutes on all the different laws I was to have memorized. "So, what're you up to?"

My mom took her dowel and pressed it down on the wooden beams that enclosed her roses. "These darn Japanese beetles. Every year they just about ruin my roses." She held up her dowel, from which a smushed green-shelled bug dangled. "Got you," she muttered, flinging him off into the grass.

"Is that what you wanted to talk to me about?" I teased, squatting down beside her.

"No." She pulled off her soiled gardening gloves and touched my face. "Honey, Ms. Slater called today after school."

"She did?" My knees felt weak. "What for?"

"Well, she wanted to tell me that your performance in class has really improved and that she expects great things from you tomorrow on the math exam."

Relief washed over me. "Really?"

My mom nodded. "She said that you're raising your hand more in class, that you're keeping up with your assignments, that you're volunteering to write out homework solutions on the board. . . ."

"I've really tried, Mom. I know I wasn't doing my best before."

"We're very proud of you. You've taken on a lot of responsibilities this year, and I think you're handling them well. And setting a good example for Lindsey too."

I gave her a hopeful look. "Does this entitle me to a shopping spree at Belk's?"

My mom thought for a moment. "I'll have to consider that. But I can tell you one thing you'll be happy to hear." She beamed. "I've saved the best news for last. As of this Wednesday, you don't need to go to Brain Drain anymore. You're through!"

I fell back on my behind, not quite comprehending what she'd just told me.

"You've really made a concerted effort these past few weeks, and as I said, your dad and I are really proud of you. I called him at the hotel as soon as I hung up with Ms. Slater, and he agreed that you could stop. We know you didn't want to go to that tutoring center, but see?" My mom patted my hand. "It was all worth it!"

"Wow. It went so fast," I said slowly. I knew I'd worked long and hard, but I could remember my first session with Chad like it was yesterday. Was that really several weeks ago?

"Don't you want to see how I do on my exam before ending my sessions?" I asked, stalling for tutor time.

My mom shook her head. "We didn't want to make you suffer any longer. Dad and I are sure you'll do well." She brushed some dirt off her legs and snipped off a few dead rosebuds. "Chad was certainly worth what we paid him."

"Yeah. I guess he was," I said. Chad had made the past few weeks of my life the best. I couldn't imagine not seeing him anymore.

What was I going to do?

"Hello. Is Chad there?"
"Speaking."
"It's Shauna. Shauna Phillips," I added, just in

case he had any other Shaunas calling him up.

"Hi! What's going on? I'm so thirsty . . . I think it's from the pepperoni on the pizza."

"Yeah. Their meat is pretty spicy." I swallowed. "Great news," I said, trying to sound happy. "Ms. Slater called my parents and told them how much I've improved in math class."

"That's great!" The warmth in Chad's voice traveled over the phone lines and into my heart. "I told you you'd prove my best student yet."

"She, um, specifically mentioned you as being the reason."

"Wow. I don't think Slater's ever done that in her life. But you're the reason, Shauna, not me," Chad insisted modestly. "You put in a lot of hard work at Brain Drain. I'm sure you'll pass that exam tomorrow with flying colors."

"Well, speaking of Brain Drain, that's kind of why I'm calling." I cleared my throat. "My parents said I don't have to go anymore. They're really happy about all you've done for me."

I nibbled on a shiny white fingernail. Maybe Chad would still want to hang out. We were sort-of friends now, weren't we? But *I* didn't want to be the one who suggested it. If Chad wanted to get to-gether, that would be cool. If not, then . . .

"That's really great," Chad said after a few mo-ments. "I knew you had it in you, and now you're proving how smart you really are."

Silence again. "And I know how much cheerleading means to you," he went on sincerely. "Now you won't have to spend three afternoons a week boring yourself at Brain Drain."

A sinking feeling swirled around in my stomach. Was that how Chad had seen our time together? As three boring afternoons a week? "Yeah," I said coolly. "I'm really relieved to put this whole math nightmare behind me. Not that it was a total drag, of course, but . . ." I drifted off.

"I hear you," Chad said. "You'll have more time to hang with Tommy now too."

"Right," I enthused. But lately the notion of spending more time with Tommy's friends, at Tommy's games, or waiting for Tommy after school had kind of stopped sending my heart into orbit. Even stranger, I'd found myself obsessing less over Tommy . . . and more over Chad! *Tommy is your boyfriend. Chad is your tutor. Get a reality check, Shauna.*

"Anyway . . ." Chad let the sentence hang.

An uncomfortable pause that seemed to last forever dangled in the air between us. "So I guess we'll just see each other around, huh?" I said finally.

"You know where to find me three days a week," Chad quipped.

"Yeah," I said, a nervous laugh stuck in my throat. "See you." Hanging up the phone, I picked up *Connected Mathematics* for one last look. A note written on green graph paper fluttered out of the book and down to the floor. Puzzled, I picked it up. In between gold #1 stickers there was the following neatly handwritten poem, in block letters:

132

Hey, Shauna.
It's my time to say—
Your challenge may be tough,
But I wish you luck today!
You've got to show your stuff to Slater,
You're the best pupil now and later!
So give it up for your tutor, Chad,
He knows his stuff and his method's rad!

I shook my head, laughing out loud. Chad definitely would not make a living writing cheers, but his sweet attempt warmed my heart. Carefully I folded up the note into a small square. I'd keep it with me during the test. With Chad's encouragement and my drive, nothing could stop me.

The air-conditioning sent a sudden chill through my body. I wrapped my comforter around my legs and stared out into space. Last night I had dreamed a terrible dream. I was sitting in one of the wobbly desks in Ms. Slater's room, taking the math test. Except I was the only student in the room.

The test consisted of one question:

Let A represent "Shauna likes Tommy."
Let B represent "Shauna likes Chad."
If Shauna likes Tommy, then she cannot like Chad.
If Shauna likes Chad, then she cannot like Tommy.
Using symbolic form, prove that the
two statements are logically equivalent.

"I can't do this!" I protested, staring at Ms. Slater. But she wouldn't let me go until I did. I'd tried and tried to solve it, but I just couldn't seem to get it right. I'd woken up frantic, my sheets clammy with sweat.

Maybe it wasn't a dream at all, I realized.

Maybe it was my life.

And maybe I was going to have to choose.

Twelve

Chad

SLOWLY I REPLACED the phone in its cradle, swallowing the bitter taste of disappointment that had bubbled up in my throat when Shauna had told me the news. Sure, I was happy for her. She'd worked really hard, and she deserved to get some good results. And I knew that coming to Brain Drain had been the last thing she'd wanted to spend her time doing.

But what about me?

For the past few weeks I'd been trying to work up the nerve to broach the subject of romance with Shauna. Specifically, romance between me and her. Believe me, I'd be the last person on earth to try and break up a happy couple. But from the little things Shauna said and did, I could tell that she wasn't one hundred percent content in her relationship with Tommy Jansen.

I thought back to the times I'd seen her in the

hall with him or by his side after a game. Shauna would be smiling, but there was a strain about her face, as if she was trying hard to please rather than relax and be herself.

Feeling downer than down, I opened my desk drawer and pulled out a piece of scrap paper covered with scribbles. I know it sounds silly, but I'd started saving the sheets of paper that Shauna had doodled on during our sessions. They made me feel connected to her in some way. I was always trying to find some hidden meaning in her marks, as if she'd written me a note in secret code and all I had to do was unearth it.

This particular paper was covered with daisies, triangles, and little *X*s and *Y*s. I was just about to shove it back in the drawer when my eye caught a tiny heart down at the bottom of the page. Two neatly intersecting lines were drawn inside: the letter *T*.

Angrily I crumpled the paper up in a ball and flung it at my door. I would never, ever have a chance with Shauna Phillips.

"Chad, I skipped social studies this morning. Can you tell me what the assignment was?" Chrissy Talbot asked me.

"Yeah, sure," I told her, quickly thumbing through my notebook and reciting the information to her. I didn't want to be rude, but I'd been standing outside room 211 for five minutes, and I didn't want to miss Shauna.

I knew I was an idiot. But after all we'd been through together, I couldn't let Shauna take this math test without being there afterward to find out how she did. Not that I had any doubts about her performance; I was sure she was going to kick butt. Finally Shauna had gotten serious about math, and there was no question she could pull this off. I just wanted to be there to be sure. *Just doing my tutorly duty.*

The bell rang, signaling the end of third period. I shifted my weight from side to side, trying to stay relaxed. My body was tensing up for some inexplicable reason. I glanced around for signs of Jansen, but thankfully the guy was nowhere to be found. I'd be able to spend my last minutes with Shauna in peace.

Suddenly the door burst open, and students began to stream out into the hall, some with happy looks on their faces, others with heads hung low. I craned my neck, trying to locate Shauna.

"Chad!" Shauna raced over and threw her arms around me. "What are you doing here?"

"I just wanted to see how the test went," I said clumsily, shuffling from toe to toe as we broke apart and I got a good look at her. She looked stunning, wearing a pair of plaid checked pants and a pale yellow sweater, her hair twisted back in a knot at the nape of her neck. "I couldn't stop thinking about you."

"Chad, it was just like you said," she bubbled. "I got in there and sat down, and when Ms. Slater passed out the tests, I took a deep breath, picked up my pencil, and *attacked!* Not only that, but some of the problems were exactly like the ones we went over last time!" She pulled out a piece of scribbled loose-leaf paper from her notebook. "Here. Slater let us keep our scrap paper. See?" She pointed to the work she'd done for several logic proofs.

I scanned it. "Looks perfect, Shauna. I think you did it!"

Without warning, Shauna flung her arms around me again. "Thanks, Chad. Thanks for everything," she whispered, burying her face in my neck. "And that note you left me was so sweet."

I hoped that she didn't hear the pounding of my heart, but it seemed much too loud to ignore. The girl of my dreams was in my arms and I held on for dear life, the tart, appley smell of her hair tickling my nostrils and the soft fuzz of her sweater sticking to my sweat-filled palms.

"Yo, Shauna."

We broke apart. There stood Tommy Jansen, his eyes shooting question marks at Shauna and daggers at me. "What's going on?"

Excitement drained from her face. "I was just thanking Chad for helping me prepare for my math exam. I really think I did well." She tucked a misbehaving lock of hair behind her ear. "It was hard, but—"

Tommy slung his arm around her shoulders. "That's great, Shaw," he interrupted abruptly. "I told you it wasn't anything to sweat about. You and your parents just worry too much." He bent over and, his eyes flicking in my direction, gave Shauna a kiss on the lips. "Come on. We're outta here," he said, ushering her down the hall. With a helpless glance over her shoulder Shauna waved good-bye.

I stood there mutely, feeling like a fool. Then anger began to seep through my body. How dare he treat Shauna like a child!

I watched them disappear through the doors at the end of the hall, trying to figure out what Shauna saw in him. Okay, maybe Tommy had his good qualities. But he definitely wasn't right for her. I was sure of that, deep in my girlfriendless heart. So why couldn't Shauna see it too?

Feeling depressed and scraggly and worthless, I trudged down the hall. I needed some man-to-man advice. And although I'd never thought I'd see the day coming, I knew who I needed to talk to.

I needed Jamie.

The rain had just started to fall when I pulled into the long, winding driveway of the Palmetto Sands golf course. By the time I got to the clubhouse, I was soaked.

"Is Jamie Manning around?" I asked the guy at the front counter, my teeth chattering.

"I think he's in back, covering up the golf carts with a tarp. Have a seat. He'll be back in a minute."

Driving winds of rain began to pelt the clubhouse windows, and I watched as golfers, their hats blowing and golf bags bouncing, ran for cover. It had been a pretty dry fall, but when we got a storm like this one, it was serious.

A loud crack of thunder shook the walls, causing the people who'd come inside to look at each other with relieved expressions that they'd made it to shelter in time.

"Well, you picked a great time to stop by," Jamie said. He dropped into the chair next to me and handed me a fluffy white towel. I wiped my face and wrapped the towel around my shivering shoulders. "Weather reports didn't say a thing about rain today. The management's going to be annoyed—they're going to have to issue a lot of rain checks today."

"Rain checks for the rain?" I laughed. "Funny, I never knew where that expression came from."

Jamie cocked his head at me. "And you're the smart one?"

I sighed. "The smart one? No, I don't think so. Definitely not." I told him what had happened over the past few days, from the great time Shauna and I'd had at Broadway at the Beach to the end of our study sessions at Brain Drain, concluding with the love fest that had gone on between Shauna and Tommy that day in the hall.

Jamie drummed his fingers on the table. "So you've come to me for advice."

I nodded.

"Man, you must be serious."

I nodded again.

"Well, you say that they were hot and heavy in the hall today."

"No," I said slowly. "Not exactly. I mean, Tommy was all bossy and Shauna just kind of went along with it."

140

"Did she look unhappy?" Jamie pressed.

"No, I wouldn't say that."

"But she'd just dominated on her math test," Jamie pointed out. "So of course she's not going to look unhappy."

That was true. "But I still don't know what to do!" I exploded.

"Give her something," he suggested. "Girls dig that. You know, a bouquet of flowers, a Hallmark card. Even just a walk on the beach."

"Nah." I shook my head. "Shauna doesn't see me that way. I'm her tutor. If I give her something, it needs to be educational. You know, tie in with the kind of stuff we've been doing." I nodded, liking my idea. "That'd be the best thing."

"You sure?" Jamie looked unconvinced. "It's my experience that the frillier and sappier it is, the more girls like it. You know, flowers, perfume, cheesy CDs."

I thanked Jamie, but I didn't want to hear another word.

I knew I had the perfect idea for a gift for Shauna. Something she'd always remember me by.

Thirteen

Shauna

"CELEBRATING MY MATH test" didn't mean quite the same thing to me as it did to Tommy. I was thinking along the lines of him giving me a small but meaningful bouquet of flowers . . . a gushy Hallmark card . . . or even just the two of us taking a drive to the beach. Tommy, apparently, was not thinking along those lines.

Instead we spent fifteen scintillating minutes discussing the upcoming Falcons–Raiders game with Lance and John: the strategies they'd use, the Raider butts they'd kick, the anticipated weather forecast (mild, with a possible chance of showers in the late evening). Next we popped by the biology rooms to turn in one of Tommy's papers and made sure to say hello to three of the prettiest girls in the junior class along the way. Then, to cap it off, we ended the day on the exciting note of stopping at Tommy's favorite sports store, where he picked up the always romantic jockstrap, a new mouth guard, and some athletic socks.

"Anyplace else?" I asked wearily, staring at the fat drops of rain that plopped on the windshield of his car. We shouldn't have even been out driving in this kind of weather—a car in front of us had nearly skidded right off the road.

But alas, soon we were pulling through the drive-in at McDonald's.

As Tommy placed his order Chad's face kept popping into my mind.

Chad was so different from Tommy. Chad was a writer of corny cheers and thought-provoking math problems who appreciated moments in the oak grove and feeding the fish. Unlike *others,* Chad had waited outside my math class because he cared about me, not because he happened to be walking by and realized it would look bad not to acknowledge something his girlfriend was so obviously excited about.

I suddenly realized that the answer I'd been looking for was a no-brainer.

Despite my total attraction to Tommy, it was Chad whom I'd shared sparks with all along. Chad, Chad, Chad! The writing had been on the wall, but I just hadn't bothered to read it.

And as I sat there with Tommy's Arch Deluxe in my lap, his greasy fries in my hand, and his large Coke spilling over on my small one stuck precariously in the cup holder, I realized it was time to end things with Tommy.

"Tommy, we need to talk," I said, straining to be heard over the pulsing beat of the radio.

"Huh? Did you say something?" He turned the knob down, and I could now hear the soothing *pat-pat* of the rain as it landed on the sunroof.

"Yes—we need to talk," I said again.

"We'll be at your house in a minute. You said you didn't mind holding the stuff."

I lowered my eyes and took a deep breath. "No. That's not what I meant."

"Then what?"

I looked away—out the window—as we sped by the fast-food places and garish T-shirt shops that lined Highway 501. "You and I are additive inverses," I told him in a soft but clear voice.

"What's that?" Tommy asked.

"Two real numbers whose sum is the additive identity zero."

"I'm a little lost," Tommy said, exasperation creeping into his voice.

"I—I think we should stop seeing each other."

Tommy's jaw dropped. "What?"

I squeezed my eyelids shut, so tightly that I began to see colors. "I don't think we should go out anymore."

"Shaw, what's wrong?" Tommy asked, his fingers clutching the steering wheel. "You sound like you're breaking up with me."

"I am," I responded in a tiny voice. I felt a lump start to form in my throat. I'd never broken up with anybody before, let alone someone I'd crushed on as hard as I'd crushed on Tommy. *You could be making the biggest mistake of your life. . . .*

"You've got to be kidding me." Tommy shook his head in disbelief. "Didn't we just have an awesome day together? We hung out with Lance and John and the gang, we—"

"No, that's just it, Tommy. Those are your friends. Your interests. I'm just your girlfriend who tags along. Who watches you acknowledge the waves from your loyal subjects."

Tommy sighed. "I'm supposed to change my life because of you?"

We drove down to my block in silence, Tommy's foot barely touching the brakes at the stop signs that lined the streets. Tears—of anger, of sadness, of all my pent-up emotions—began to well up in my eyes, and I blinked to keep them back. He drove right past our make-out spot and pulled up in front of my house. Thankfully Lindsey wasn't outside.

"Tommy, I liked you for so long," I said, not caring how weak or desperate it made me sound—it was the truth. "Then I finally got you. And it was great."

"Shauna, let's forget this whole conversation, okay?" Tommy said, his voice cracking. "You're tired, you—"

I wiped away a tear. "I'm tired of putting every bit of energy I have into you. That was a big math exam I passed, Tommy. It meant a lot."

"That's what this is about? Some stupid math test?" He slammed the dashboard with his palm. "I was there to congratulate you!"

"It's much more than that." I paused. Tommy

wasn't an evil person. . . . He had his flaws, sure, but so did everybody. I'd just been so hung up on his looks that I hadn't bothered to figure out that on the compatibility scale, we were football fields apart. "We're just not right for each other. Being your girlfriend isn't how I expected it to be."

"Shauna, I—"

I reached out to shush him. "You're still the same gorgeous guy I was crushing on. But we're not—we . . . we never really connected. At least not in the way that I think you're supposed to connect with a boyfriend," I said, barely believing I had actually spoken the words out loud. "I'm sorry."

Tommy looked over at me, his face a mixture of sadness and anger. "Is there someone else?"

I toyed nervously with the bracelet on my left wrist. "Not exactly."

Tommy's eyes narrowed. "It's that wimp of a tutor you've been seeing, isn't it?"

When I didn't say anything, Tommy laughed coldly. "I can't believe this. What kind of crap did he put into your head?"

"This isn't about Chad," I said firmly, anxious to get out of Tommy's car before I changed my mind. I deposited his burger and fries—wrappers intact—on his lap and got out, not caring if the rain soaked me to the skin. "It's about us." A small lump was forming in my throat. "I'll never forget all the good times we shared."

Tommy's jaw hardened as he shifted the car into drive. "You know where to find me if you change your mind," he said finally. Without another word he spun out into the wet street.

Clutching my books to my chest, I let the tears mingled with raindrops fall freely down my face. They weren't so much tears of sadness as they were tears of relief—relief at doing what my heart had been telling me to do for the past few weeks. I felt as if the weight that had been pressing down on my shoulders had finally been completely lifted.

And as I stared down at the reflection of my face in a newly formed puddle, I thought of another face. The face of the person I now knew I was really meant to be with.

The sweet, kind, adorable face of Chad Givens.

"So you finally did it," Holland said into the phone.

"Finally?" I repeated, snuggling into my thick terry cloth robe. I sank my chilled body down to my bedroom floor.

"This was a breakup waiting to happen," Holland declared. She sounded so definitive. But then, that was Holland.

"I still feel sad about Tommy, though." I sniffled.

"Yeah, all right, the guy's a looker. But he's so caught up in his own natural charisma that he didn't even have time to notice all your great qualities. You're better off without him."

"I know." I rolled over onto my stomach. "Holland?"

"Yeah?"

"There's someone else I'm crushing on."

"Chad Givens."

I almost dropped the phone. "How could you know? I didn't know for sure myself until today."

Holland laughed. "Shauna. You're *always* on cloud nine when you come home from a tutoring session. Chad, Chad, Chad."

I groaned. "Is it that obvious?" I stared up at the ceiling. "How shallow am I? It hasn't even been an hour since I broke up with Tommy and I'm already planning my next conquest."

"Just as shallow as everyone else at Fletcher," Holland teased.

"Thanks a lot."

"Anytime." She laughed.

I began to pace the room. "Seriously, Hol. How do I get Chad to like me?" I demanded. "He's not like other guys." I waved my hands around in the air abstractedly. "He—he's into educational stuff. Tutoring. Math."

"Well, what do you like about him?" Holland prompted. "The way he factors an equation?"

"Duh! No! It's everything about him. How he's so sweet and gentle." The more I thought about it, the more I began to realize just *how* much I liked Chad. How could I have been so blind for so long? "He's not my boyfriend, but he takes the time to show me he cares. And he's funny too, when you get to know him." I took a breath, getting into it. "And his eyes, Hol, his eyes are the deepest, choco-latey brown with these little golden flecks in them and—" I stopped talking then because I could hear

Holland tapping her nail on the telephone receiver.

"You've already sold me, Shauna. I'm a sucker for sweet and gentle."

I sighed. Sure, Tommy was chiseled gorgeousness, with a face that would help him sail through life on a wave of admiring glances. But Chad was good-looking in a different, more special way. Cute and rumpled. And his sweet nature, his patience, his genuineness . . . suddenly I found myself thinking he was the cutest boy in the world.

After Holland and I said our good-byes and hung up, I sat down, lost in my thoughts of Chad. If only I could make him see that life was more than just graphs and numbers and that I wasn't just his pupil . . . I was a *girl*. A romantic girl who had developed a killer crush on him. A crush that held meaning and promise.

A crush that was realer than anything I'd ever felt for Tommy.

A crush that could break my heart.

Fourteen

Chad

B Y TUESDAY AFTERNOON I was suffering from serious Shauna separation. Everything I came in contact with reminded me of her: the smell of green apples in my kitchen fruit bowl, a highway billboard advertising Broadway at the Beach, even the mere mention of ice cream. After I'd left Jamie at the clubhouse on Thursday, I'd gone straight to the bookstore and picked out the perfect gift for her. I'd never bought a present for a girl before, unless you counted my mom's standing order of slippers and body lotion at Christmas, which I didn't.

I'd waited outside Shauna's locker that morning. Finally, when the first-period bell was just about to ring, I couldn't wait anymore. I'd turned to head down the hall toward my first class and *boom!*— there she was, a vision in a sleeveless flowered top and lime green pants, her hair softly waving around her face.

Suddenly shy, I'd handed her the flat, square-shaped package. "For me?" she'd asked, surprised.

I nodded. "Just a little something that I thought you would appreciate."

"A kid's book?" she said curiously, pulling off the paper and turning it over. *Math Curse*, by Jon Scieszka and Lane Smith.

"It's about this girl who's having a hard time in math class and then finds out that her whole world is one giant math problem. She's cursed, to be exact," I explained sheepishly.

"Sounds like someone I know," Shauna said wryly.

I shook my head. "Yeah, but you don't know how it ends. Read it and let me know what you think."

Shauna looked up at me. "Chad?"

Just then the last bell began to ring.

"Yes?"

The bell seemed to fluster her. "Um, I, uh, I guess I'd better go," she said, backing up. "Can we talk later?"

"Sure." I couldn't help but notice that her cheeks were practically flaming. Before I could say anything more, she'd reached the corner and had turned down the corridor.

What did she want to tell me?

I didn't run into Shauna once the rest of the day, and when I showed up at Brain Drain that afternoon, I felt a strange sense of loss as I looked over at the empty study carrel. My new pupil, freshman Ricky Korbel, had canceled because of mono. I supposed I should have used the extra time to do some homework of my own, but I just didn't have it in me.

"Are you all right?" Lizbeth Fisk asked, blowing a huge bubble with her gum. She was standing on a movable wall ladder, shelving library books. "You look a little pale."

I slumped down at one of the round library tables. Lizbeth and I had never been close, but we shared a certain sense of camaraderie. She'd worked at Brain Drain as long as I had. And she was also a whiz in math, second to me in demand.

"I'm kinda down," I confessed.

"Girl problems," Lizbeth guessed. "Let me see." She pretended to think for a minute, nibbling on a fingernail. "Could she be, oh, about five-foot six, long wavy brown hair, ruby red lips, and, um, a cheerleader?"

I snapped to attention. "How did you guess?" I blurted before I could catch myself. Man! She was good.

Lizbeth grinned. "Chad, I haven't seen you so excited to tutor someone since you were paired up with Mike Brett, the guy whose father owned that potato chip factory down in Charleston."

I sighed at the thought. "Yeah. He kept me supplied with a steady stream of sour cream and onion chips the entire time he came here."

I smiled at the memory briefly, but then remembered what we'd been talking about. "So I like Shauna Phillips," I whispered frustratedly. "Fat good that's going to do me. She's hooked on her boyfriend."

Lizbeth laughed scornfully. "That football guy?

He's got a million girls after him. They'll be history."

I frowned. "Are you sure about that?" I mean, I wanted to date Shauna more than anybody, but I certainly didn't want her to get hurt by Tommy. Or worse, I didn't want to be the guy she sought solace with on the rebound.

"Yes, I'm sure. They'll be history," Lizbeth said, sitting down with me at the table. "But Chad, are you sure Shauna's the right kind of girl for you? I mean, she's a cheerleader."

"So?"

Lizbeth sighed. "The cheerleaders never seemed like the nicest crowd to run around with."

I shook my head. "I might have said the same thing before I got to know her. But Shauna's different—she's funny, she's pretty, she's sweet. . . ."

"And beautiful," Lizbeth finished.

"She said she had something to tell me," I said, suddenly thinking out loud. "What could it be?"

Lizbeth cracked her gum. "The cheerleaders are practicing up in the gym. Why don't you drop by and find out? You're not doing any good hanging out here."

"I think I'll do that," I mumbled, standing up. I *was* dying to talk with her. Heck, why not drop by? After all, the gym wasn't out of my way or anything. The only problem was, I'd have to temper myself. Otherwise as soon as I saw her I'd be begging her to break up with Tommy and go out with me.

"Thanks, Lizbeth," I said over my shoulder, walking out the door.

"Good luck," I heard her call after me.

As I came around the bend I grimaced. Tommy Jansen and a couple of his buddies were congregated near the water fountain. I had no intention of stopping, but Tommy reached out toward me, giving me a funny look as I walked by.

"You're that Brain Drain guy, right?" he said, more of an accusation than a question.

"I guess you could say that," I said, slowing down. "I work there."

"Why've you been bothering Shauna Phillips?" he asked, his tone vexed.

"Bothering?" I repeated, confused.

"You know. Hanging around her. Calling her. That kind of thing."

I stared at him. "Uh, I think you've got me mixed up with someone else. I'm her tutor. We work together on her homework."

"Yeah, but what are you tutoring her in?" one of Tommy's friends joked, elbowing the other Jansen groupie. Tommy shot him a look that would freeze lava. The guy shut up quick.

"I'm her math tutor. So that would mean I'm tutoring her in . . . math," I said, starting to get annoyed. "But we're done," I threw in. "She's not coming in anymore."

A look of surprise flashed in Tommy's eyes. "Really?"

I nodded. "Yeah. She didn't tell you?"

Tommy ignored my question. "Well, leave her alone. She doesn't want you around, trust me."

I looked him levelly in the eye. "I'll hang out with whoever I want. If you've got a problem with Shauna, talk to her. Don't bring me in on it." Adrenaline pumping, I shoved past them and up the steps to the gym.

I inhaled deeply, trying not to get angry. I envisioned myself meditating in Master Chung's dojo, when I was in what's called Present Time. Present Time is a state of being when a person is in complete harmony with himself and with nature. When you're in Present Time, nothing can make you mad or upset. Instead you're on your way to personal perfection, completely in touch with your serene self.

I felt a little funny trying to meditate in the middle of the near empty hall, but I took several deep breaths and relaxed my shoulders anyway. Present Time was always the answer. I certainly wasn't going to let Jansen get to me.

Now relaxed again, I approached the gymnasium. Snippets of conversation drifted out into the hallway. I could hear lots of "Okay! Show that Falcon Spirit" and "Come on, Falcons. Score!" being bandied about the gym.

My hand rested on the door, pushing it in ever so slightly. The metal made a slight *thunk,* but the loud, pulsing music blasting from the gym was so loud that there was no way the cheerleaders could hear me. I definitely didn't want to disturb Shauna if she was in the middle of practice. But yet again, I was dying to see her . . . and she had acted like there was something she wanted to tell me. Would it be a bad move to go in and watch? I shook my head. That would look way too desperate. And odd. Maybe I'd just wait for her in the hallway.

Then the sound of Shauna's laughter—pretty, silvery laughter—rang out during a pause in the music. My ears suddenly perked up. I inched even closer to the door and peered through the crack. The entire Falcons cheer squad was assembled. Thick red and blue mats were pulled out on the floor, and towels, T-shirts, and megaphones lay scattered all over the place. Shauna was wearing a blue T-shirt and shorts, her face flushed. She looked different to me for some reason.

Contented.

"So you sound like you're glad it's over," a girl with curly red hair said to Shauna, pulling one of the mats out to the center of the room.

Shauna breathed out slowly. "I am, you know?"

What were they talking about—her tutoring sessions?

"He seems so nice, though," said Natalie Smith.

"It's not that," Shauna said slowly. "He is nice. But—" I strained to make out her words, but they were lost as she sat down and did a stretch.

Could *I* be the guy they were talking about? I leaned my cheek against the cold, hard metal of the door. I knew that Shauna didn't like coming to Brain Drain. But that was in the beginning, before she was privy to my sparkling wit, my debonair way with fractions, the way I handled a protractor. Sure, she'd kicked and screamed all the way, but that was before we'd started working together.

Before we'd become friends.

"And that little *gift* he gave you. I mean, please," Holland Thorpe said, her hands on her hips. "That has got to be the dorkiest thing I've ever heard of."

"I wouldn't mind having it," Natalie teased.

Shauna laughed. "It's yours."

Holland turned up the music even louder at that point, and the girls started doing a complicated and mysterious series of tumbling moves.

Feeling like I was going to throw up, I stumbled away from the doors and leaned against a locker bank, reeling from the crummy shock of it all.

I, Chad Givens, was the laughingstock of the entire Falcons varsity cheer squad.

I put my hand on my chest. My heart was still in there, beating away. I was convinced it had been lying in the middle of the gym while all the cheerleaders pounced on it one by one, letting Shauna have the privilege of giving it the final kick.

I was so *sure* she had started to like me. Was I the only one having fun when we were together? I'd thought we'd made a bond with each other. She'd acted so sweet, so kind, so interested in my every word.

So phony.

Lizbeth had been totally right. I thought of Shauna's expression when I'd handed her the book. She'd acted like she really liked it. She didn't act like she thought it was *dorky*.

It was bad enough having to confront Jansen and his moron friends out in the hall. I knew they thought they were way above me in the coolness category.

But Shauna too? How could she do this to me?

Tommy and his friends were right, I decided, beating a hasty retreat down the hallway. I was meant to be a brain. What was I thinking—that I could actually have a chance with a girl like Shauna? The prettiest cheerleader at Fletcher High? I mean, for Pete's sake, she was going out with one of the star football players. Like she'd give that up.

I was a math whiz. I was supposed to be smart. But thinking I could get a girl like Shauna Phillips to like me had to be one of the dumbest—no, *was* definitely the dumbest—thing I'd ever believed in my sorry little life.

"What are you doing, man?"

I looked up from my place on the floor. "Getting rid of my life."

Jamie picked up the cardboard box that sat beside me on my bedroom carpet. Inside was my collection of *Games* magazines, the three statuettes I'd won as the Otterburg Memorial Math recipient for three years running, my honor roll certificates, and a bunch of first-place ribbons from Latin competitions.

"I'm sick of being smart," I said, viciously ripping up a perfect math quiz from last year. "Smart doesn't get you anywhere!"

Jamie sprawled out on my bed, his muddy cross trainers making a mark on my bedspread. I didn't care. I was sick of being neat too. "Uh, Chad,"

Jamie said, "why don't you calm down and fill me in. Nothing can be this bad."

I picked up a compass and scowled. "Oh, no? Try being dissected in front of the entire varsity cheer squad. They were practically taking numbers, talking about me in practice today, Jamie. Shauna was totally making fun of me." A stab of anger jabbed me as I fumed over my ill-treatment at the insensitive hands of the cheerleaders. "They've got some nerve," I seethed. "Who do those cheerleaders think they are anyway?"

"Cheerleaders," Jamie answered wisely. "That's the point. You know the deal—us lowly guys aspire to date cheerleaders, who in turn treat us like dog meat. It's an age-old tale, Chad." Jamie sighed contentedly. "But I'm willing to live for the morsels they throw us."

"I'm serious, Jamie," I muttered, crumpling up a pamphlet titled *Polygons and You: The Lecture Series*. "I don't care if she's a cheerleader or the president of the debate club. I like her for who she is, not what she is." I put my head in my hands, feeling dangerously close to making a total blubbering fool of myself. Phil and Jamie would never let me live it down.

Jamie put his chin in his hands. "Was she really making fun of you, Chad?" he asked, a thoughtful expression on his face. "I find that kind of hard to believe. From what you've told me, it sounded like y'all really hit it off."

"I know. I thought so too." For a moment I

wondered if maybe I did have it wrong. Could I have misinterpreted the whole thing? There was always the tiny chance that Shauna had been talking about someone else. After all, she'd seemed so sincerely happy when I'd given her the book—Shauna couldn't fake that.

Could she?

Maybe I was wrong. Maybe they had been talking about another person.

I shook my head. Yeah, right. Another person Shauna was glad to get rid of so that she could get on with her life. Someone who had given her a parting gift. A dorky parting gift at that.

That dork was me.

No, I wasn't wrong. Shauna Phillips wanted me out of her popular, beautiful life. And I was going to have to see to it that I was.

Chad Givens was no one to feel sorry for.

Fifteen

Shauna

"**D**O I LOOK any different?" I asked my mom. She gasped, reaching out to grab my hair. "Don't tell me you got highlights."

I pushed away her panicked hand. "No." My mom is always worried I'm going to do something weird to my hair and screw it up. I've always kept it the same way: long, wavy, and soft, mossy brown. Ever since she got her own cut to her chin several years ago, my tresses have been her vicarious pride and joy. "The streaks are just because I've been outside a lot lately. You know how it gets." I took a deep breath. "That's not what's different."

"Then what?" my mom asked patiently.

"Well," I said dramatically, "I thought you might want to see the face of someone who just *got a ninety-two on her math exam!*" I thrust the paper in her face. "Ninety-two, ninety-two, ninety-two!" I sang.

"Shauna!" my mom exclaimed, throwing her arms around me. "That's wonderful!" We hugged.

Then I broke away. "I've got to go make a phone call." I raced down the hall to my room and pushed the speed-dial button on the phone to call Chad. I'd moved him up from number seven to number two (Holland would always be number one. If I was nothing, I was loyal).

Disappointingly, all I got was the Givenses' answering machine. I waited for the beep. "Hi, Chad, it's Shauna." I paused. "Anyway, I wanted to tell you that I got a ninety-two! Yes, that's right, you're not hearing things. A ninety-two! If you get home in the next hour or so, give me a call. I've got a lot of things to tell you. Bye."

But I guess Chad didn't have much to tell me. Because he never called back.

I ignored the curious stares at school, the rumors that Tommy had dumped me because I was quitting cheerleading, that I was moving to Florida, that I wouldn't go as far with him as he wanted me to. None of it mattered, and I knew if I didn't make a big deal of it, my moment as a hot topic of gossip would pass.

"Don't dignify these losers with a comment," Holland sniffed to me at lunch.

"I heard he's already asked Natalie Smith out," Kristen Baumgardner said, biting into her bologna sandwich and waiting for my reaction.

I took a sip of my milk. "I'm okay with it," I said. "Really."

"Shauna's into Chad Givens now," Holland informed her.

"Oh," Kristen said, looking surprised.

"How's Mark doing?" I asked Holland.

She smiled. "Excellent. He's finally done with all his college visits, and we'll get to spend some real time together this weekend."

"That's great," I said, doing my best to sound enthusiastic. But it was hard. I was happy for Holland and all, but I couldn't help being preoccupied with the fact that I'd never heard from Chad the night before.

I sighed. "Don't you think it's a little odd that Chad hasn't called me back, Hol? I mean, I've left him two messages, and he never returned either one of them." I set down my milk. "And I feel like he's been avoiding me too."

"That is pretty weird," Holland reflected. "Did you do anything to make him mad?"

"Well, if you count getting a ninety-two instead of a hundred, maybe." I shook my head. "Nope. Nothing I can think of. It's funny. I thought he'd be dying to talk to me as much as I am to him."

Then, as if he'd heard me, I saw that Chad was suddenly in the lunch line. I excused myself from the conversation and hurried over.

I didn't want to look too obvious, so I pretended to examine the selection of chips piled near the cash register.

"Hi," I said, smiling brightly. Chad looked really cute in his usual rumpled, wrinkled way. His frayed khakis were covered with pink eraser fragments and he wore a white Henley rolled up at the elbows.

Chad barely looked at me. "Oh. Hi."

"I wonder how much these things are selling for," I said, holding up a bag of fat-free cheese curls.

"I wouldn't know," Chad said brusquely, moving up in the line. "I'm not a walking calculator."

I forced myself to laugh. "Who said that you were?" I responded lightly. I reached forward and touched his arm. "Did you get the message I left you last night?" I asked. I couldn't figure out why he was acting so strange. Almost rude. Had Holland been right? Did I actually do something that made him mad?

I brushed that thought aside. No. That couldn't be it. Maybe he'd been out late or something, that's why he hadn't called me back.

"Yeah, I got it. I was out." He handed the cashier a couple of dollar bills.

I tried to catch his eye, but he turned his head, making contact impossible. "I—I just thought you'd be more excited for me," I said, my voice quivering like the Jell-O that sat on Chad's tray. "You were so encouraging before the test and all, and—"

"I'm happy you got a ninety-two, Shauna," Chad said quickly as he took his change and shoved it into his pocket. He fumbled with the napkin dispenser. "Look, I'd love to talk with you, but I've gotta run. See ya." Before I could say anything else, he bolted to the other side of the cafeteria, apparently to sit with the friends he'd been with at the football game.

Humiliated, I hurried back to my table, my eyes brimming with tears.

This was completely out of character for Chad. He had me more confused than any math problem ever did.

What had gotten into him?

Several days later I spent most of sixth-period English trying to come up with answers. Not that I was missing much in class by spacing out. That day, just like the past eight days before, we were discussing *Hamlet*. In addition to reading the play in class, I'd seen the Mel Gibson–Glenn Close movie and the Kenneth Branagh release too. This, I'd decided, made it acceptable for me to tune out Mr. Ferne and turn my attention to more pressing matters: specifically, how to get Chad to notice me.

After much discussion Holland, Kristen, and I had come to the same conclusion: Chad was suffering from a severe case of I-need-a-girlfriend-but-I-just-don't-know-it blues. We all agreed that Chad liked me. If I'd learned anything in our tutoring lessons, it was logic. And reason showed that Chad was meant for me and that I was meant for him. His weird behavior only indicated that he was deeply confused. From what he'd said, Chad had never had a girlfriend. It was understandable that he'd feel a little uncomfortable around a girl who was so obviously into him as I was, even though I thought I was being completely low-key about the whole thing.

I chewed on my pencil. Subtlety definitely

hadn't worked. I guessed Chad's brain didn't function like other guys' did. Realistically it probably worked better. But when it came to girls and love, he just wasn't too quick on the uptake. I'd made sure we'd crossed paths in the hall. I'd waved at him when I spotted him standing in the front lobby before school started. I'd even left him an anonymous note in his locker that read *Someone close to you really likes you. Signed, Hopeful.*

Nothing. Not one sign of interest. Not one sign that he'd even been aware of any of my efforts.

I thought back to how Chad had looked at me the day before my exam, when I was visualizing in my math classroom. There had been such kindness in his chocolate brown eyes, they had seemed to speak directly to my soul. We had definitely made a connection over the past several weeks. I knew it, and there was no way Chad could persuade me otherwise. Actions speak louder than words.

"Shauna? Are you with us today? Or is your mind on some other prince besides the prince of Denmark?"

Several students tittered. I blushed, putting my pencil down on my desk and focusing my attention on my teacher.

Then it hit me like a lightning bolt. Not paying attention in class back in September was what had gotten me a front row seat with Chad. What brought Chad and me together in the first place could bring us together once again! I'd blow off math for a week, I'd need a tutor . . . and voilà! Instant Chad! My grades wouldn't suffer for too long—just long enough to meet up with Chad and get our relationship on track.

Turning my attention back to that deranged Ophelia, a smile appeared on my lips. There was definitely no way I was going to let a total sweetheart like Chad Givens slip out of my fingers.

After all, I was a Fletcher Falcons cheerleader. This was no time to sit on the sidelines.

Sixteen

Chad

JAMIE INSISTED ON taking me out to cheer me up after my tae kwon do class on Saturday morning. More literally I took him out, since he was still careless and licenseless. But it was the thought that counted, I guess.

I'd just been going through the motions since the day I'd heard Shauna dissing me in the gym. Nothing had been able to pull me out of my funk. And I didn't want to be pulled out. This was my first true love, and I wanted to be left alone to wallow in the disgusting depths of pain, to really feel what it was like to have your heart trampled on and dished up like a bowl of lumpy mashed potatoes.

And Shauna's pathetic little attempts to humor me did nothing but burn me up inside even more. She'd passed by me in the hall at least three times a day. She'd waved at me when I was hanging out with Phil in the front lobby before school started.

What was she trying to do, show the other cheerleaders what an idiot she could make of me? Playing mindless little head games? I swore I wouldn't succumb to her superficial charms.

To make matters worse, Lizbeth Fisk had even gotten in on the scene, leaving me a stupid note in my locker that read *Someone close to you really likes you. Signed, Hopeful.* Now *that* was dorky. I rued the day I'd ever mentioned my futile crush on Shauna to Lizbeth—she *would* make a joke out of the entire situation.

The past several days I'd been as cool as a cucumber to Shauna, rebuking her every phony effort, every insincere gesture, every hopeful glance. But on the inside I'd been a basket case. And Jamie, being the true friend he was, made it his mission to bring me back to the world of the living.

So we did what guys did. We went to the mall, to the used CD exchange, to Phil's house. We washed my car. Then we just drove around. And all around us were girls: salesgirls trying to entice us into trying something on at the mall, college-age girls winking at us in cute little sports cars before speeding off, girls with tanned legs wearing short shorts—in October!—walking along the boulevard.

To Jamie's dismay none of them turned my eye. Truthfully they turned my stomach. One thing I'd learned was that I was a one-woman kind of guy. If I couldn't have Shauna, I didn't want to have anybody else.

At least until the pain went away.

Finally we ended up at the Riverboat Café. As usual Emmy came over to our table and plopped down a basket full of steaming hot hush puppies and a crock of butter.

She cocked her eye at me. "Hey, buddy. What's the matter? You look lower than low."

"He's lost his cupcake, cupcake," Jamie divulged.

"Oh, baby." She patted my hand. "Let me get you guys some fries, pronto. If you're going to be miserable, might as well do it over a full stomach."

"Chad, you're scaring me, bro. Talk to me," Jamie begged me a little while later as we left the restaurant and coasted along the highway. "There's got to be some way I can cheer you up. How about the beach?"

"The beach," I repeated apathetically. "Fine." It was all the same to me. Mall or beach, my broken heart and I traveled anywhere.

I glanced out the window as I drove. The day had started in a perfect complement to my mood: overcast and dreary, heavy gray clouds spreading across the sky. But now, to my annoyance, the sun was starting to make an appearance.

"See, Chad?" Jamie said, trying to appease me. "Even Mr. Sun wants you to be happy."

I growled as I pulled into the beach parking lot.

We stepped out of the car and headed toward the sand. You might not think many people would be on the beach on a late October afternoon, but you'd be wrong. It was actually pretty crowded. Not with girls in bikinis or anything (thank God), but with old geezers holding metal detectors that buzzed at any speck of dirt remotely resembling a coin, older couples holding hands, and families with small kids trying to convince themselves that the South Carolina summer wasn't really over.

"I'm about ready to admit defeat," Jamie said, breaking the silence as we walked down the beach. "You've got it bad, Chad."

"You're not telling me anything I don't know," I replied sadly, stepping over a pile of clamshells someone had collected, then deserted.

"But she did break up with Tommy, right?" Jamie asked.

I nodded. I'd heard that from someone in one of my classes, and I was pretty sure it was true. I think even Shauna herself had mentioned it to me on one of our encounters in the hallway, but I was pretty much blocking out her voice. I couldn't figure out why she thought I'd care—or why she kept trying to bump into me. Hadn't she done enough damage already? It was like she was going out of her way to be nice to me, to try and talk with me. Girls. Who could figure them out?

Jamie and I walked several miles, climbing up over boulders slimy with seaweed and jumping away from the waves that threatened to soak our feet. The wind was sharp—it always was down by the water, and I shivered, wishing I'd worn more than just a long-sleeve cotton shirt. As the afternoon wore to a close we sat down on the sand, making sure we were out of the water's reach.

"I'm sorry, Chad," Jamie said. "I didn't help you very much, did I?"

I smiled at him. "You were great, pal. You did cheer me up."

"Really?" Jamie asked, his eyes widening.

I couldn't lie. "No." I patted his back. "But thanks anyway."

Jamie's face fell. "Well, you could have let me think so."

"Now I'm the one who's sorry." I stared down at the strip of hotels behind us. The smaller, family-owned hotels had started to be replaced by bigger, giant ones to satisfy the ever growing tourist demand for new facilities. Bigger was better! Newer not older! Remodeling was going on up and down the strip. I stared at one nearby hotel that was covered with scaffolding. It was a huge pink building, and on its side was a worn-out-looking mural of the ocean. Huge sections of paint were missing, eroded by years of salty ocean air. Construction workers were overrunning the place, barking out orders and raising booms and platforms.

The SeaSpray, I realized with a jolt. The hotel that Shauna's dad ran.

For a moment I thought about telling Jamie and suggesting that we go over there. I didn't know why—it wasn't like Shauna was going to be hanging out at the pool taking a dip or anything. And I didn't want to see her anyway. I just thought it might be nice to see the place her dad worked in. To even meet her dad—he hadn't been home for dinner that night I ate at Shauna's.

Then I decided against it. I'd feel too silly, and what if Shauna was there? I turned back around to look out at the water, the waves frothy with whitecaps.

The ocean mural had provided me with a valuable lesson. The workers weren't trying to salvage the mural they had . . . they were going to create a whole new one.

Love was kind of like that too. Sometimes you had to start from scratch.

Seventeen

Shauna

I PRACTICALLY SKIPPED into Brain Drain on Monday afternoon. "Hi," I trilled to the tall blond girl behind the desk. I recognized her from before. "I'm here to see Chad Givens."

After over a week of not doing my homework and skipping a few classes, my math grade had—as I'd predicted—gone down. Way down. A tiny part of me felt bad. I'd worked so hard to bring my average up. When I got a seventy-two on my last quiz, I was irritated. I knew I could have easily pulled a ninety if I'd studied. But when my parents announced that they thought I should go back to Brain Drain for a few more sessions—"maybe we were too hasty, dear"—I was the happiest girl on earth.

Or at least I was until the bombshell hit me.

"Chad?" The blond girl looked confused. "He's not scheduled to work today," she reported, checking the tutor schedule posted on the wall.

"He's not?" Disappointed, I sagged against the counter. "Are you sure? There must be some kind of mistake. See, I was a student of Chad's for practically a month."

The girl nodded. "Yeah. I know who you are."

"Oh. Well, anyway, my grades kind of took a little nosedive, and my parents sent me back here for more help." I made a face. "Gotta get those grades back up there."

"Good. I'm glad to hear you've got the right attitude." I watched, perplexed, as the girl picked up a pen, pencil, and a binder full of paper. "Let's get going."

I stood rooted to my place. "No," I said, trying to clear up her obvious misunderstanding. "Chad's supposed to be my tutor, right? We had a great rapport."

The girl sighed. "Well, I hate to break it to you, Shauna, but you're stuck with me. You were supposed to get Chad again. That's normally how it's done—once paired together, always paired together." She looked me apologetically in the eye. "But Chad requested a switch."

The rest of the day was a giant blur. Lizbeth finally sent me home since it was obvious that I wasn't paying attention to a single word she said.

I felt completely, utterly devastated. This was the final blow. I'd been kidding myself all along, trying to convince myself that Chad really *did* like me but was too shy/too smart/too reserved to

175

make a move. But the bitter truth was that he just wasn't interested.

Chad must have really thought I was stupid. He didn't even want to tutor me anymore. I was that hopeless. *He wants someone with a brain. Someone like Deb or Lizbeth.*

That night was one of the worst nights of my life. And I made sure everyone in my family knew it.

"Dad, tell Shauna she can't play 'Blue' anymore. She's going to wear out the CD!" Lindsey whined.

"That's what songs like that were written for," my dad explained gently, shooting me a loving, sorrowful look. He swept Lindsey up in his arms and carried her out into the kitchen. "How's about we leave Shauna alone for a while, huh? I'm in the mood for a homemade milk shake. . . ."

I hunched over in my chair and stared ahead, not really seeing the wall unit in front of me filled with family photos, my mom's glass collectibles, the TV. I felt like smashing them all to pieces so that the shards could even further rip my heart.

I'd never felt so lonely in my life.

Despite my better judgment, I showed up on Wednesday for what I knew would be a tortuous tutor session at the hands of Lizbeth Fisk. It was pretty pointless, really. The whole point of getting a tutor was to be close to Chad again, and since that was turning out to be one fat flop, going to Brain Drain was just part of the failed attempt at winning Chad's heart. My parents had paid for a week's worth of sessions, though, and I felt guilty letting their money go to waste.

Lizbeth was waiting for me at the door. "Why don't we study in Chad's carrel? You probably feel right at home there," Lizbeth suggested.

"It doesn't matter," I mumbled, feeling a lump form in my throat. "Wherever."

We sat down, and I listlessly handed my homework and book to Lizbeth. By now I knew the whole routine.

She whizzed through the pages. "Looks like everything here is right!" she exclaimed, peering at me.

"Really," I said tonelessly, staring out the window. I wanted to be anyplace but there.

Lizbeth coughed. "Here. Try these work sheets. Then I'll be able to see where your weaknesses are. You know, help you focus on what really matters."

What really matters is that Chad Givens wants nothing to do with me and I don't know why. I couldn't feel much more miserable than I did at that very moment. Blinking back tears, I read through the problems. When I got to number three, I stopped. I'd done the same problem with Chad. Quickly I wrote out the answer to that one and all the rest. I passed my paper back to Lizbeth. Then I rose to my feet.

"You might as well know," I said, trying to hold it together. "I made my grades go down on purpose. I understand all of my homework and everything that appears on these work sheets."

"So you're just a masochist, is that it?" Lizbeth asked.

"I—I'm in love with Chad Givens," I blurted, tears threatening to spill down my cheeks any second. "But he's angry with me about something. He won't have anything to do with me, and believe me, I've tried. I thought that if I came back to Brain Drain, he'd have to speak with me. But then you ended up as my tutor, and everything's ruined."

"Sorry," she said dryly. "I didn't mean to stand in the way of true love."

"You're not standing in the way of anything," I choked out. "Chad wants nothing more than to be out of my life. And he's doing a great job of it."

Lizbeth handed me a tissue from her purse. I blew.

"Thanks for trying to help me today," I said thickly. "But this is something that Brain Drain can't fix."

I trudged down the blocks to my house. The leaves had just started to change their color, and the few that had fallen crunched under my hiking boots as I walked in heavy, miserable steps. Summer was my favorite season, but I loved autumn as well. So many great things normally came along with it: rising a notch in the pecking order at school, new classes, new friends and activities.

The lump in my throat became a full-fledged sob as I thought about this. I'd made such a mess of the school year, and now I'd have almost seven more months to live with my mistake. Why had I wasted so much time with Tommy when Chad was right under my nose? I'd been so blind.

An acorn skidded past me, bouncing along the

sidewalk. Stupid squirrels. Couldn't they see a person was trying to walk alone in misery? Then another acorn whizzed past me, this time in the air.

I spun around. There, with a goofy grin on his sweet face, stood Chad. "Shauna, wait up!" He jogged over.

I couldn't speak. I couldn't breathe. *Chad.*

"Shauna," Chad said, coming to a stop. He took my limp hands and gave them a reassuring squeeze. "We've got a major misunderstanding here."

"We—we do?" I stammered stupidly.

"I just came from Brain Drain. Lizbeth told me what happened today."

Now not only was I completely distraught, I was humiliated as well. "I wish she hadn't done that." I sniffled, looking around for a vacant manhole to jump into.

"Why? She's the one who told me how you really feel . . . ," Chad whispered, his voice trailing off. He reached up and gently touched my face. "She—she said that you said you . . . you were in love with me." Normally Chad's face turned red when he was embarrassed, but right now his cheeks were about as pale as a bar of Ivory soap. "Is that true?"

"Well, I—I—"

"I've never known Lizbeth to lie." His voice was shaky.

A tear slid down my cheek. So what if I did love him? It wasn't any use. It wasn't like he was going to say—

"I feel the same way."

I gulped. "You do?"

"You're all I can think about, Shauna. Meeting you was the best thing that ever happened to me. And ever since you've been gone, I haven't been able to see straight."

"But you've been avoiding me," I mumbled, not meeting his gaze.

Chad sighed. "I was just hurt. And a little confused too."

"Why?"

"I heard you talking to the cheerleaders at practice last week. About how you were glad to get rid of me." He paused, searching my face for an answer.

I looked back at him. Now I was the confused one. What was he talking about?

"How you told them you were glad it's over," Chad continued, staring into my eyes. "That really hurt."

I wiped a tear away. "Tommy," I said slowly, the realization of what had happened suddenly hitting me. "Tommy," I repeated with conviction. "We were talking about my breaking up with him." I threw my hand to my mouth. "You thought we were talking about you?"

Chad's beautiful eyes clouded over, making me want to throw my arms around him. "But how do you explain the gift, then?" he asked, the emotion audible in his voice. "The dorky gift? What's that all about?"

I giggled. "Tommy gave me a five-by-seven

glossy of his football picture the day after we broke up. I found it in my locker." I laced my fingers in Chad's, flooded with relief and happiness. "You thought I meant the book you gave me?"

Chad nodded.

I stooped down and picked up an acorn. "I'd love this acorn if it were a gift from you," I told him, realizing it sounded completely cheesy. But it was the truth.

"I've got a better gift to give you than that," Chad whispered softly. He wrapped his arms around me and bent his face to mine. When our lips touched, I felt my heart plunge down to my toes and bounce back up again, all warm and glowing. This is what I'd been missing all along.

This is what having a boyfriend was supposed to feel like.

That afternoon, for old times' sake, Chad and I did a math problem together. Neither of us knew what the answer would be. But it was going to be a lot of fun finding out.

S. P.
+
C. G.

Do you ever wonder about falling in love? About members of the opposite sex? Do you need a little friendly advice but have no one to turn to? Well, that's where we come in . . . Jenny and Jake. Send us those questions you're dying to ask, and we'll give you the straight scoop on life and love in the nineties.

DEAR JAKE

Q: *I like this guy at school, but I heard he's not interested in me. What do guys look for in girls?*

AV, Raleigh, NC

A: Well, let's see. You have to be exactly five-foot four, and you must have straight hair. Oh, and you'd better like U2 and hate Mariah Carey. That sounds ridiculous, right? That's because there is no one set of traits that makes a guy interested in a girl. Every guy has different tastes. Of course, there are certain qualities that are universally appealing. If you're friendly, approachable, and you laugh at our jokes and make a few of your own, then you're in good shape. It's also important that you have confidence in yourself and remember that there's a guy out there who will be happy with you exactly as you are.

Stop worrying about who or what you *should* be and

just enjoy being you. And don't listen to what anyone tells you about that guy you like; rumors are as reliable as your big brother's promise that he won't read your diary.

DEAR JENNY

Q: *Mike, my boyfriend, is probably a dream come true for most girls. He's supersensitive, and he always wants to spend time with me. The problem is, I like to be alone sometimes. It's not that I don't love Mike—I do. But sometimes I just want to be by myself. What should I do?*

LP, Wheaton, MD

A: Everyone needs their own space. Some people need more than others, and it sounds like that's the case with you and Mike. When you're part of a couple, you need to balance the time you spend alone and the time you spend together. If you do love Mike—and it sounds like you do—let him know that while your commitment to him hasn't changed, you do need some breathing room in order to stay sane. If he loves you, he'll understand. Devoting time to yourself is one of the most important things you can do. And you'll be a better girlfriend because of it.

Q: *I always want everyone I care about to be friends with each other, so I was happy when my boyfriend hit it off with my best friend. However, they get along so well that sometimes I* *feel like I'm the one who doesn't belong. Is it wrong of me to want them to stop spending so much time together?*

ST, Fairfax, VA

A: I'm amazed that you're dealing with this situation as well as you are! Most girls wouldn't be putting up with this at all. It's mature of you to accept their friendship, but it's also understandable that you would like things to cool off a little between them. It's possible that this is an innocent friendship and they will both understand when you tell them—individually—that you'd rather they spent less time with each other and more time with you.

But if they continue to grow closer and neither of them listens to how this makes you feel, you have a more serious problem on your hands. Unfortunately many girls have lost their guys to best friends. It could be terribly painful to be betrayed by the two people closest to you, but if they do get together, if they do hurt you like that, they aren't worthy of your friendship in the first place.

Do you have questions about love? Write to:

Jenny Burgess or Jake Korman
c/o Daniel Weiss Associates
33 West 17th Street
New York, NY 10011

Real *life.*
Real *friends.*
Real *faith.*

Introducing Clearwater Crossing—

where friendships are formed, hearts
come together, choices have consequences,
and lives are changed forever . . .

#2   0-553-57121-4

#1   0-553-57118-4

*clearwater
crossing*

Bantam Doubleday Dell
Books for Young Readers

BFYR 160

Watch out
Sweet Valley
University—
the Wakefield
twins are
on campus!

Jessica and Elizabeth are away at college, with no parental supervision! Going to classes and parties . . . learning about careers and college guys . . . they're having the time of their lives. Join your favorite twins as they become SVU's favorite coeds!

Look for the SVU series wherever books are sold.